THE BOTTLE STOPPER

Angeline Trevena

Bogus Caller Press

ISBN: 978-0-9934864-0-1

Cover art: Ben Farrow
Cover art copyright © 2015 Ben Farrow
www.estragonhelmer.com

Published by Bogus Caller Press
www.boguscallerpress.co.uk

Publisher's note:
The Bottle Stopper is a work of fiction. All names, characters, and places are the product of the author's imagination, used in fictitious manner. Any resemblances to actual persons, places, locales, events, etc. are purely coincidental.

ALSO BY ANGELINE TREVENA

Cutting the Bloodline

THE HEAD

THE KEEP

THE
EYE

NEWSTONE

□ □ □ □ □

THE BAYS

□ □ □ □

THE
BIRCHES

THE WILLOWS □

THE BEECHES
□ □ □ □

HEIGHT STREET

SALT STREET

FORGE STREET

THE GARDENS

HAVERHEAD

LYNSTOCK

THE LAWNS

BUCK WAY

SILK LANE

SATIN
SQUARE

WASH STREET

FOLD STREET

BRIDGE
LANE

THE
WATCH

THE HOPE

THE COMPOUND

COMPOUND STREET

EYE STREET

TONGUE STREET

TOP STREET

NAVEL STREET

HUNG STREET

OVERLOOK

THE WALL

DUTIES

SECOND STAIR

THE
HIDE

THE DONNS

CRICK LANE

HIND STREET

OVERLOOK

THE WALL

THE SLIP

THE FLOOR

THE EDGE

DONNSTRIDE

THE CUBES

THE CUBES

THE SQUEEZE

THE EDGE

FALWERE RIVER

1

Maeve felt her stomach lurch. She pressed her lips together and swallowed the bile back down. Breathing through her mouth, she dragged a sack, stuffed with damp rags, from the corner of the storage room. Positioning it in the centre of the space, she sat down, and crossed her legs.

To her right was a pile of glass bottles, not one the same as another. There were blue bottles, green, brown, clear, the occasional yellow. They were different sizes, some were round, some square. The only bottles she was instructed to discard were the ones marked with the word 'Poison'. Apparently, it was bad for business.

To her left was a pile of equally mismatched corks. After years of practice, she could quickly judge which cork would fit which bottle; matching them like unsuspecting participants in an arranged marriage. At least, in the slums, that was something she'd never have to worry about.

Also within reach, was a crate of plant cuttings to push into the bottles. Some were nothing more than riverside grasses, others were flowers, weeds, twigs, lavender. The odd few were actually herbs, but Maeve couldn't identify them. Nor could she identify whether any of the plants were poisonous. Their purpose was merely aesthetic. If people were lucky, they would get a sprig of wild garlic or mint. Something that may help to disguise the vile taste of the medicine itself.

In front of her was a barrel containing Uncle Lou's miracle medicine. Proven to cure any ailment from the common cold to broken bones and irregular heart rhythms. This was the source of the stench that turned Maeve's stomach. Little did Lou's customers know, it was nothing more than water from the putrid river that flowed past the slums.

Uncle Lou's apothecary shop stood along The Wall, under the imposing shadow of the cliff face that rose up behind. Further along the street, the buildings parted for the rough staircase that cut its way through the rock, and up to the next level of the city. The buildings along The Wall, leaning casually back against the cliff, were the oldest in the slums, having stood there for several generations. And while they were a mismatched row of hodgepodge buildings, built by hand from found materials, they were a far cry from the shacks that sprawled before them. Their bricks weren't a uniform colour, their windows didn't match, and you could easily point out the extensions and alterations that had been made over the years. But they boasted such luxuries as electricity, and indoor toilets.

As Maeve filled and stoppered each bottle, she stacked them into a small wheeled cart. It was only after much begging that her uncle had supplied her with it. It was a child's toy, the kind that usually carried wooden bricks. Maeve wondered which unwitting child he'd stolen it from.

She dragged the cart through to the kitchen, the bottles chattering as they jostled for space. She shushed them, gently easing the cart over the pits and dents in the wooden floor.

She could hear her uncle in the shop which occupied the front of the building. A small hall joined it to the back of the house, split into the kitchen and storage room on the ground floor, Maeve's bedroom and a bathroom above, and Uncle Lou's bedroom in the attic space. Every room was small and cramped, the staircases steep and narrow.

Maeve crept across the hall and crouched on the bottom stair. She enjoyed listening to the different voices of the customers, and catching glimpses of them through the glass-panelled door that joined the hall to the shop.

It was easy to distinguish which level of Falside the customer came from. The strength of Lou's phony French accent was proportionate to the weight of his customer's wallet. The richer customers were served with bottles from the top shelves. The contents were, of course, identical, but the bottles were fancier, and sold at a higher price.

"Madame, can you ever truly put a price on

your poor father's health?" Uncle Lou was saying. "Your father, who has raised you, protected you, and chosen for you so wisely. Does he not deserve the best? The most potent, and fastest working medicine? Do you not want him returned to you as soon as possible? Think of your children, and how much they would miss their beloved grandfather. Imagine explaining to them that he had died because you wanted to save money."

After a moment, Maeve heard the chink of coins. She watched as the young woman stepped in front of the door. She wore a high-necked pale blue dress, her blonde hair drawn up in an intricate weave of plaits. In her gloved hands she held a tiny blue bottle. Maeve remembered it, there were vines and grapes embossed around the neck.

Maeve picked up her own long braids, and twisted them up over her head. As she released them, they dropped back down heavily. Her dull hair was escaping in places, tufting out like marsh grass. The ends were tied together with old pieces of string. She sighed.

She looked down at her own tattered gloves. Goodness knows where Lou had found them. She'd cut the fingers off herself to allow for a better grip on the bottles. There was a sizeable hole on the palm of one, and she picked idly at the loose threads.

"My life will never get better," she whispered to herself.

Leaning forward, Maeve lifted a vase of dried flowers from a side table, and slipped the grubby table cloth out from under it. She ceremoniously laid it over her head like a veil, standing slowly, her head bowed reverently.

"I do," she whispered, extending her finger for the ring. She snatched her hand back. "But not to you, you fiend."

She looked up at the ceiling and spun around. There was a large ceiling rose above her, the sort that should host an impressive chandelier, but this one had never had so much as a bare light bulb hanging from it. She span around and around, faster and faster.

"I will marry for love!" she called out as she stumbled. She scrabbled for the table, but fell onto her knees, bashing one against the edge of a loose floorboard.

The door to the shop flew open, and Uncle Lou's sharp nose poked through the gap.

"What the hell are you doing?" he demanded. "I'm trying to run a business here, trying to keep a roof over your head. I don't have to, you know. Too much trouble, and you'll end up just like your crazy mother." He stabbed the air with a bony finger. "Now, shut the hell up." The door slammed shut.

Maeve turned and wandered up the stairs. She gently closed her bedroom door behind her, and climbed onto her bed. Leaning on the small window ledge, she gazed out over the muddied slums beneath her, and across the Falwere River beyond.

2

Maeve woke to a familiar sound. Above her, a woman giggled, high-pitched and shrill, while Uncle Lou's bed thudded and squeaked in rhythm.

It was still dark outside, and the moonlight pooled on Maeve's bed like milk. She knelt up and watched the moon's reflection fracture on the surface of the river.

She rubbed at her wrist. She'd been dreaming again. She could still feel the ghost of her mother's fingers locked around her arm, the burn as she was wrenched away. Maeve had only been six years old, and she clung onto every memory she still had of her. Her hair, her voice, her smell. Her strange stories. Her screams as they dragged her away.

It didn't feel like eleven years had passed since.

Stepping down onto the cold floor, Maeve tiptoed to the door and opened it a crack. She winced as it creaked. She slipped through the narrow gap and made her way downstairs, expertly avoiding any stairs that squeaked.

In the kitchen, she found some left over ham,

just a few slices which were beginning to harden at the edges. She found some bread and, after shearing off the stale end, cut herself two slices and pressed the ham between them.

There was a large jar of mayonnaise on the table, and Maeve unscrewed the lid to breathe in its scent. Her stomach rumbled at the eggy smell. The sauce had separated slightly, and Maeve stirred it back together with a knife. She spread a generous helping into her sandwich. She couldn't remember the last time she'd had mayonnaise.

Carrying her food through to the shop, she settled herself onto the cushioned window seat. There were only a few lights outside, a few houses where people were up early for work, or late after a night in the bars or brothels.

Maeve didn't hear Uncle Lou until he reached the hall, his companion falling down the bottom few stairs.

"Get up," Lou hissed. "And get out."

Maeve pressed herself into the corner.

They came into the shop, Lou helping the woman stay on her feet. Her dress was unbuttoned, revealing a stained corset beneath. Her tangled hair had come unpinned, and she gripped her scuffed boots in her hand. She twisted around, and lay her cheek on Lou's bare chest.

"Don't throw me out darling," she slurred, stroking his face with her spare hand. "Make love to me again."

"That was not love."

"Please, Louis."

"I'm finished with you." He pushed her away, and she stumbled backwards, knocking bottles from the shelves as she scrabbled to save herself from falling. She collapsed onto the floor, sitting amongst the broken glass and stinking river water.

"Now look what you've done!" Lou grabbed her by the hair and dragged her, screaming, to the door. He unbolted it and threw her out.

"You owe me!" she squealed.

He threw a handful of coins at her. "The rest will pay for the broken bottles." He shut the door and bolted it. The door thudded as she threw something against it. Lou muttered something under his breath and disappeared back upstairs.

Maeve looked out of the window and watched the woman, now carrying only one boot, limp down the steps in her stockings.

She listened to the house for a while, but it seemed Uncle Lou had gone back to bed.

She collected the dustpan and brush from the kitchen, and swept up the broken glass as quietly as she could. She found old rags and mopped up the spilt water, turning her head away from the stench.

She unbolted the front door and retrieved the woman's discarded boot. She put everything into an old flour sack, and stashed it in a corner of the store room to dispose of later. Uncle Lou didn't like to wake to evidence of the night before. This way, they could all pretend it never happened.

When Maeve finished bottling for the morning, she

found the front door wide open, and the shop filled with the smell of the slums. Uncle Lou was leaning on the railing outside. She stepped out next to him and looked down at the street below.

The wind pushed its way along The Wall, grabbing at women's skirts, and threatening to steal hats. It also carried with it the angry voice of a small, red-faced man. He threw his arms around above his head, screaming into the face of the young woman who ran the flower shop next door. The scene had drawn quite a crowd.

"She's getting evicted," said Uncle Lou.

"Not paid her rent?" Maeve asked.

Lou nodded. "Times are hard."

The landlord marched up the steps into the shop, reappearing with a bucket of flowers in each hand. Despite the woman's pleading, he deposited them both over the railings into the mud below. He went back into the shop, and came out with two more.

The woman sobbed as she watched her livelihood slap into the thick sludge.

Lou shrugged. "Landlord could rent that place ten times over. It won't be empty for long." He patted his hand against the railing. "Just be glad this place belongs to me."

Maeve looked up at him, searching his face for even a flicker of emotion. His expression didn't change. He'd inherited the property from his late wife, passed to her from her father.

Lou's father-in-law had cursed their marriage right up to the day he died, labelling Lou as a 'money-grabbing, lazy, good-for-nothing.' Lou hadn't relished the idea of taking over the old man's cobbler business, despite it having been there for almost half a century. The profession required too much skill, and too much hard work. But Lou's wife wanted to honour her father's memory, and refused any changes Lou proposed. It hadn't been long until she disappeared. The subsequent hunt had uncovered only her shoe, half buried in the silt of the river. Her death was assumed to be an accidental drowning, and everyone moved on with their lives.

Within two days, the cobbler's shop had reopened as an apothecary. Lou claimed the change was vital for his own emotional healing. The scent of the shoe leather held too many painful memories.

"Let's just hope a respectable business moves in," Lou said. "We don't want some charlatan bringing down the reputation of The Wall." He snorted, laughing at his own joke. He turned and went back into the shop.

Maeve sat down, dangling her legs between the railings. She watched the crowds disperse now that the excitement was over.

The florist glanced up as she passed by, her face swollen and blotchy, her mouth set hard. Women in Falside knew to let things go; hysterics usually ended in a one-way trip to The Compound. Even in the slums, they felt the gaze of the administration's eye.

Maeve remained there for most of the

afternoon. When customers came, she kept her eyes on the floor as she had been told. She watched a workman remove the florist's sign from its ironwork bracket. When the sun sat low above the river, bathing Falside in the deep orange glow of evening, a wagon pulled up to the shop next door, dragging its wheels through the mud.

Maeve clambered to her feet and pushed the shop door open. "Uncle Lou, the new tenant is moving in."

He pushed past her, and folded his arms across his chest.

A man and woman climbed out of the truck, dragging baskets and boxes from the back. Standing on a box, the man hung his sign from the empty bracket.

"A bakery," said Uncle Lou. "Well, at least it's something respectable." He huffed and disappeared back inside.

The woman returned to the wagon for more boxes. She looked up at Maeve and smiled brightly, and Maeve couldn't help but smile back.

3

Maeve packed the last of the bottles into the cart and dragged it into the kitchen. She closed the door to the storage room, and leant against it for a moment to catch her breath.

Lou appeared in the doorway, rapping his knuckles against the door. Maeve jumped.

"Are you out of bottles?" he asked.

Maeve nodded.

"You need to get some more. There's a bug going around Falside and I'm only half stocked out there. I can't have important customers seeing my shop half empty."

"Perhaps you can increase the price because of low stock."

Uncle Lou moved quickly, grabbing her plaited hair and pulling her towards him. "I am increasing the price, you clever little thing, but I still need stock to sell. You do the labour, and leave the business planning to me." He released her. "Now go out and get some bottles. And get me some small, pretty ones."

Maeve rubbed her head, the ache beginning to

spread through her skull.

She grabbed her cardigan from the back of a chair and pulled it on, carefully rolling up the left sleeve. She pushed her hands into the deep pockets, her finger finding the familiar hole in the lining.

Stepping out into the sunshine, Maeve trotted down to the steps and skipped over onto one of the planks of wood that served as a more desirable walkway than the bare mud. Through the drier months, the mud dried solid, ploughed into deep troughs and ruts, threatening to sprain or snap ankles with every step. In the wetter months, it served only to ruin clothes and steal shoes.

She ran along the planks with practised assurance. She could almost navigate The Floor with her eyes shut, and she knew all the best places to get bottles. The bars for larger, plainer bottles, the delicatessen for tall, slender ones, the dispensary for unusually shaped bottles. But today, she would have to climb the rugged steps up to The Hope, where a small perfumery stood in Crick Lane.

Crick Lane was wide and bright, each shop flying a colourful canopy above its window. The shop doors had small, delicate bells above them, and they chorused together as women, with little better to do with their day, idly browsed in and out of them.

Despite being just a few months from her eighteenth birthday, Maeve was small and slight, looking no more than thirteen at best. She moved along the street completely unnoticed.

She slipped up a narrow alley beside the perfumery and leaned casually against a gate a few feet from the shop's back door. She knew the routine of everyone who worked there, and waited for the owner's daughter to sneak outside for a quick cigarette.

The woman appeared, nodding quickly to Maeve in a silent understanding of discretion. Women weren't given credits to buy cigarettes, nor were they supposed to idle in alleyways.

The woman lit a half-burned cigarette with shaking hands, and sucked on it as if it were the only thing keeping her alive. A voice sounded from inside and she winced, flicking the cigarette to the ground. She smoothed down her white apron, fixed a pin in her hair, and disappeared back inside.

Maeve wandered over and picked up the still smouldering cigarette. She placed it between her lips, the end greasy with lipstick, and sucked. Her mouth filled with smoke, and she coughed. She stubbed the cigarette out on the wall, adding to the speckling of soot marks, and dropped the butt into her pocket.

A man walked up the alley, his cap pulled low and his collar turned up to his jaw. He carried a waft of beer and urine with him. Maeve pressed herself against the wall, dropping her gaze to the floor. She held her breath as he passed. She glanced after him, and watched as he shook a blade from inside his sleeve. Maeve looked back at the ground, counting to forty before looking up again. The alley was empty.

Maeve exhaled, and turned her attention back to the perfumery.

Rising onto her toes, she peered through a small window into the dim interior. There was no one in the back room, and six pretty bottles stood on the counter.

As Maeve nudged the door open, a full range of scents reached her, ranging from delicate and floral, to heavy and spicy. She closed her eyes and breathed them in, imagining the exotic places each scent came from. She couldn't believe any of them were native to Falside.

She inched the door further open, and slipped into the cool room. She kept her eye on the door to the shop, and listened for the muffled voices beyond. Creeping across the flagstone floor, she lifted the bottles, one by one, and carefully lowered them into her pockets.

Looking around, she spotted half a cheese loaf. She wrapped it back into its paper, and tucked it under her arm. She took one last deep breath, trying to lock the smells into her memory.

As she slipped back outside, she heard the door to the shop open. She flattened herself against the wall and slid down into a crouch.

"Goddammit!" A man's voice.

The back door swung open, slamming into Maeve's knees, and shuddering back from the impact. Maeve bit her lip against the pain.

Four thick fingers wrapped around the edge of the door, and the man leaned out. A wrinkle of fat cushioned the base of his bald head. He looked up and down the alley, while Maeve held her breath behind the door.

"Goddammit!" he yelled again, and disappeared back inside. "How many times have I told you to lock that damn door? You'll pay for those bottles, girl." After a moment, he yelled again. "Goddammit! And my bloody bread."

Maeve stared at the floor, and slowly counted time away in her head. When her heart had returned to its usual rhythm, she pushed her hands into her pockets, wrapped her fingers around the bottles, and walked casually away.

She came back onto Crick Lane, and followed it to The Downs. She turned towards the stairs that would take her back to the slums. Then she stopped. She had no reason to hurry back.

She looked around her, opting for the security of another alleyway, this time running past the monastery, and joining The Downs to the large, open square of The Hide. The alley was dark and narrow, made even narrower by the boxes and crates that were piled there.

Maeve looked up at the small windows of the monastery, the stained glass scenes barely visible through layers of dirt.

Up ahead, a small door opened and a monk, dressed in his black habit, stepped out. Maeve froze, unsure what to do. She had never met a monk before and wasn't sure of the proper etiquette, especially when she had no business creeping around the back of the monastery.

She tucked herself in between the boxes as the monk looked up and down the alley. She held her breath against the acrid stench of rotting food and dead rats.

The monk tugged a woman into the alley. Her hair was matted, her unbuttoned dress revealing the ridge of her angular collar bone. Her skirt was hooked up on one side, revealing her laddered stockings, and her thigh above. A slum girl.

She grabbed the priest roughly, kissing him hard. His hand moved up to her blouse, slipping between the buttons, kneading her flesh.

She pushed his hand away and stepped back with a toothy grin. "Now, now, Father Harris. No freebies." She held out her hand.

The monk pressed a few scrappy credits into her palm. She looked at them with a scowl.

"You know I'm worth more than that."

"We both know you're not."

She snorted, pushing the credits into her pocket. "I'll tell everyone." She jabbed him with a bony finger. "Everyone will know what their church donations really pay for."

"And who's going to believe a cheap whore?"

She snorted again and set off down the alley. She stopped and turned back to him. "My pimp's gonna get you." She spat out a large globule of phlegm. "You'll be back."

The monk shrugged. "Yeah, probably." He stepped in through the door, and pulled it shut behind him.

4

Maeve loaded the last of the bottles onto the shop shelves, and clambered back down the step ladder. She stood back, and checked for any obvious gaps. On tip-toes, she shifted a few bottles around until she was satisfied with the display.

Lou strode into the room, pulling his coat on.

"I'm going out," he said. Maeve could already smell alcohol on him.

She nodded, struggling to fold the wooden ladder. It slipped from her grip, slammed to the floor, and set all the bottles rattling.

"Careful!" Lou barked. He grabbed the ladder and stashed it behind the counter. "Try not to break anything while I'm gone." He crossed to the front door and pulled it open. "Or I'll bloody break you."

The bottles shook again as he slammed the door behind him.

Kneeling on the window seat, Maeve pressed her nose against the glass and watched Lou disappear into the darkness of The Floor. In her lap, she moved her fingers into an obscene gesture.

She switched off the lights and slipped out of the front door. She hurried down the steps to the street, and straight up those of the bakery next door.

The last few loaves, pies, and pastries were still laid out in the window, nestled into wicker trays and baskets. Maeve's mouth watered, and she swallowed hard. The sign in the door had already been turned to 'closed', but as Maeve pushed the brass handle, it swung open and she stumbled inside.

A woman turned to look at her. Her cheeks were red, and dusted with flour. Her hair had come unpinned and strands frayed around her face. She smiled broadly, her green eyes lighting.

"I'm afraid we're just closing," she said. "But I'm sure I've time to serve one last customer. What can I get you?"

Maeve inhaled the scent of sugar and warm bread. As she closed her eyes to appreciate it without distraction, her head spun, and she realised how tired she was. She snapped her eyes open again.

"I'm from next door. My uncle owns the apothecary."

"Ah, of course." The woman extended her hand for shaking. "I'm Gretta."

Maeve slipped her hand into Gretta's, allowing it to be shaken up and down. "Maeve."

Gretta moved back to the counter, grabbing a chocolate éclair from the rack. "It's a little floppy, but it'll taste just as good." She slipped a napkin around it and held it out.

Maeve stepped back. "I don't have any money."

"It's free. Whatever isn't sold gets wasted anyway. Take it."

Maeve took the offered pastry in both hands. She knew the names of all the delights bakeries sold, but she'd never tasted any of them. Not that she could remember, at least. Uncle Lou's diet was mostly liquid, so he never stocked more food than the absolute barest of essentials.

The moist chocolate topping clung to Maeve's teeth as she sunk them into the light, air-filled pastry. Soft cream slipped over her fingers, and she let the taste sit on her tongue for some time before swallowing it down.

"So, is it just you and your uncle?" Gretta's question brought Maeve back to the room.

She nodded, licking cream from her lips.

"How old are you?"

"Seventeen."

"You're only two years younger than my daughter."

Maeve nodded again, speaking with her mouth full. "I didn't see her when you arrived."

"She came along after. I believe the last tenant drew quite a crowd when she left."

Maeve shrugged. "Not a lot happens around here. Gossiping and delighting over others' misfortune are the favourite pastimes."

Gretta laughed. "Don't worry, I've lived on The Floor long enough to know all about gossip."

Maeve sucked her fingers, her eyes wandering over the remaining cakes.

"Don't get to eat cakes often?" Gretta asked.

Maeve shook her head.

"How about another? I have these cakes topped with mint chocolate. They're not a huge seller, but they're my daughter's favourite."

Maeve took a step back and gestured towards the door. "I should get going."

"Is your uncle waiting for you?"

"He's out for the night, but..." Maeve looked at the floor.

"My daughter's out with her dad. They've popped back to our old shop in The Squeeze to pick up the last of our stuff. They won't be long. You could wait to meet them if you like. I could put the kettle on? Better than going back to an empty house."

Gretta and Maeve quickly made their way through a large pot of coffee and half a tub of biscuits. Maeve's cheeks ached from laughing, and this carefree happiness was a feeling she wanted to keep hold of. But she knew the shadow of reality wasn't far away.

The bell above the door jingled, and cold air from outside rushed in. Gretta put down her mug and hurried over to relieve her daughter of a large box. Behind the box was the same contagious smile as Gretta's, the same eyes. Maeve smiled back instinctively.

"This is my husband, Hex, and our daughter,

Topley," said Gretta, placing the box on the counter. "This is Maeve. She lives next door."

Topley was slim and athletic, her hair cut short. She wore a hooded jumper and jeans turned up at the bottom. Maeve had only seen a handful of women in trousers, and all of those had been manual workers. Topley wasn't just unconventional, she was defiant. Maeve liked her instantly.

Hex shuffled across the floor, balancing his box on one huge forearm while he shook Maeve's hand. His fingers were thick and hairy, his palm rough.

Topley skipped across the floor and pulled Maeve into an unexpected embrace. "Welcome to the family," she whispered in Maeve's ear.

Slipping her hand into Maeve's, she led her out of the shop and into the hall behind. The house was an identical layout to Uncle Lou's, but it was brighter here, fresher, happier. It felt like what Maeve had always imagined a home should feel like.

They tumbled onto Topley's bed and giggled.

"Can you stay over?" Topley asked, propping herself up on one elbow.

"I have to be in bed before my uncle gets home."

"Where's he gone?"

Maeve knotted her fingers behind her head and sighed. "He calls it his 'rhythmic exercise'." She rolled her eyes. "He's at the brothels."

"Well, don't you worry, you'll always have a safe place here. I just know we're going to be great friends."

Although Maeve didn't dare say it aloud, somewhere in the ball of warmth growing in her stomach, she knew it too.

5

Lou picked his way along the wooden walkways, tentatively making his way down to The Edge, where the Falwere River sucked at the slums like a hard-boiled sweet. The stench was almost unbearable and Lou pulled his handkerchief from his pocket to cover his nose.

He'd been born in the wet silt of the river, the son of a clam digger who thought nothing of how his fingers reeked. It was only through Lou's quick tongue that he found his status improved to live along The Wall. It wasn't easy to make a move like that; a man's past could cling to him stronger than the mud here. Drag him down.

But he always found himself back here, walking the horribly familiar route down to the brothels of The Slip. The women there were ugly and gristly, but they were cheap, and up for anything. And they treated Lou like a king.

"Louis!" came a shout from ahead.

He stopped, raising a hand to shade his eyes from the glare of the lit doorway.

"Who's that?" He stepped closer, and his face

broke into a grin. "Lilly," he sung.

She leaned against the doorway, her dress barely covering the bits he paid for.

"I missed you, Louis." She stepped forward, running her hands down the lapels of his jacket.

"Is that right?"

Hooking her fingers between the buttons on his waistcoat, she pulled him against her, gazing up at him. She smiled, revealing a few gaps where teeth should have been.

"I've missed you so, so much." Her breath stank of fish and beer. "Are you coming in?"

Lou nodded and allowed Lilly to lead him inside.

6

Father Harris sat in his small room staring at the papers in front of him. The names and dates had blurred together some time ago. He rubbed his eyes and leaned back, reaching out for his wine.

"Crap," he said, as the glass tipped, staining the papers pink. He snatched them up and shook them, drops of wine dripping from them like blood. "Oh crap."

Laying the papers out to dry, Father Harris shifted his chair to the window. As one of the longer-serving monks, he was honoured with a view of the monastery's walled garden.

It was by far the largest garden on The Hope, and it was reserved exclusively for the small population of monks. The high walls ensured that barely anyone even knew it existed. It was a true oasis.

It was beautifully landscaped, and enjoyed an exotic array of trees, shrubs, and flowers that seemed to have been specifically chosen for their fragrant quality. Harris could enjoy it without needing to leave his room. The far corner held a small cemetery for monks who had passed on over the last century or so. The monastic lifestyle did seem to be one that afforded its members an unnaturally long life. Perhaps it was something in the water.

Harris pushed himself to standing and wandered over to his wardrobe. He pulled the door open and knelt down. He pushed the habits aside and felt the back for the loose panel. Easing it out, he laid it aside and reached into the gap. He removed a large, brown bottle, cradling it carefully.

"There you are." He eased out the cork, and lifted the bottle to his lips.

The home-made brew was brutally strong, and Harris had barely drunk half before his arms refused to lift the bottle anymore. Leaning back against the cold wall, Harris fell asleep, snoring loudly.

A knock at the door woke him. His body ached from the cold, and his joints retaliated with pain as he rolled onto all fours and crawled towards his bed.

"Father Harris?" came a voice through the door.

"Go away!" he yelled, wincing as the sound pounded his brain. He eased himself up onto his modest mattress, and sat with his head dangling limply.

After a moment, the voice came again, more hesitantly this time. "Father Harris?"

Huffing, Harris forced himself to his feet, and stumbled to the door. He pulled it open. "What?" he snapped.

Brother Grant jumped back. He was young, still wearing the pale grey habit of a novice. "I'm sorry, I —I—I just..." He gestured helplessly down the corridor.

Harris held up his hand. "My apologies. I had some bad brew." He attempted a smile, but it didn't soften the fear on the novice's face. "I guess it's all bad brew really."

Brother Grant smiled warily. "I guess so."

"What can I do for you?"

"There's someone asking for you. A woman. A lady. You know, a—" He lowered his voice to a whisper. "Prostitute."

Harris nodded, keeping his face serious. "Yes. Yes. She's probably here for a reading lesson."

Brother Grant shot his eyes to the ceiling. "Probably."

Harris stepped into the corridor and closed his bedroom door. "You need to relax a little. Why don't I see if she has a friend who you can teach to read?"

"No, no, thank you."

"Maybe she can teach you to read." Harris laughed, walking away towards the church.

Lacey was stood by the altar, her face tilted up to the impressive cross that hung above it. Her blonde hair was illuminated in shades of pink and green as the sunlight caught it through the stained glass window. If it wasn't for her low-cut dress and her bare thigh, she would have almost looked angelic.

Harris crept across the flagstones, keen not to disturb her moment of peace. He wanted to remember her like this. As he sat down on the front pew, the wood beneath him creaked, and she turned. The image was lost.

Lacey smiled and settled herself next to Harris. He reached up to touch her face, but she shied away.

"It's too dark in here for sunglasses," Harris said, reaching out again.

Relenting, Lacey let him remove her glasses. They were too big for her; designed for a man.

Her eyelid was sunk over the empty socket, a crescent of red flesh showing beneath it. Harris ran his hand gently over her cheek. He would never forget seeing her at his bedroom door, her face unrecognisable; swollen and bloody. He had scooped her up, run through the monastery, paced the room while Father Benson carefully removed her eye. And he would never forgive himself for it.

But she had never complained, or cried. She had sat quietly as Father Benson cleaned her wounds, and strapped her broken fingers. When he had finished, Lacey had thanked him for his mercy.

Harris had no doubt that she had said the same to her pimp after he disfigured her.

"Come on." Harris stood and held out his hand. Lacey slipped her calloused hand into his. She stood, and followed him to his bedroom.

"Sit down," Harris said, gesturing to the bed. "Are you warm enough?"

She nodded.

"Let me get you some food."

When Harris opened the door, Brother Grant was stood outside, his face guilty.

"Eavesdropping?" Harris asked.

Grant's face flushed, his mouth opening and closing uselessly.

"Walk with me." Harris set off towards the kitchen, leaving Grant to skip a few steps to catch up. "You've been here long enough to know what's going on. That church out there is a front, a mask, a lie. All this is a lie." He gestured to the building around them. "All this is a lie." He plucked at his habit. "We stand there every week and tell the good citizens what not to do, and then we do it all. We perform marriages with terrified brides, brides forced to marry a man they don't, and probably will never, love. Do you know how many of them I've seen on a Sunday hiding bruises? Because us men, despite the uniforms we wear, despite the titles we have, we do as we please. In this city, we are kings. And those women, they're nothing but our property." He stopped, and turned to Grant. "Did you know that I have a daughter?"

"I didn't," Grant stammered.

"I'm not the only one." He started walking again. "Falside is a pit, a drain, a latrine, full of immorality and sin, and this is the centre of it all. We're the source of the virus, and we're spreading it everywhere."

"Are we talking about syphilis?"

Harris sighed. "We're talking about everything. Look, I may be drunk, but I can promise you this:

whatever reasons led you to the monastic life won't mean shit in a year's time. You'll have forgotten them. I haven't a clue why I joined."

"It's not all corrupt." Grant stopped walking, and looked up at Harris. "Is it?"

"We're put here by the administration, and they —well, you're better off not knowing what they're doing." He patted Grant on the shoulder. "But there's always hope."

Harris nudged his door open with his hip, and hurried across the room to relieve his hands of the hot bowl of stew. He set it down on his desk, laying a knob of bread next to it.

He turned, and found Lacey asleep on his bed. He sat down on the edge, and brushed her hair back from her face. She stirred, and slipped her hand into his.

"Sorry, I didn't mean to wake you," Harris said.

"Don't worry, I wanted to speak to you."

"Eat first." Harris passed her the food and watched her eat as if it were her first meal in a week.

"You're too kind to me," she said between mouthfuls.

"Nonsense. I wish you'd let me do more for you."

"You know you can't. He'd never let me go."

"So what are you going to do? Just wait for him to kill you?"

Lacey lifted the bowl to her lips and drained it. She wiped her mouth with her sleeve. She looked down at the floor.

"I'm pregnant."

Harris opened his mouth. He scrabbled for something to say—something supportive, something positive—but he knew what this meant for her. A one-eyed prostitute was a curious oddity, maybe even a fetish. But a pregnant one was a financial liability.

"I need money so that I can fix this," she said. "I don't have anyone else to ask."

"Does he know yet?"

Lacey screwed her hands together.

"He did this, didn't he? Your pimp got you pregnant."

Lacey nodded. "He told me to sort it."

"I'm a monk, Lacey, I don't have any money."

She wiped away a tear. "I don't have anyone else I can ask."

Harris thought for a moment. "How much do you need?"

"Two hundred."

"I'll get it, somehow. I'll work it out. Until then, you can stay here with me."

"I can't. If he finds out, he'll kill us both."

7

The sky was already beginning to lighten when Maeve heard Uncle Lou trip up the stairs outside. The shop door opened, then slammed shut. Bottles breaking. Swearing. More stumbling on the stairs. As the footsteps passed her room, Maeve held her breath and tightened her grip on her blanket. She relaxed as he tripped up the stairs to his room. Two bumps as he kicked his boots off, then the creak of his bed.

Maeve crept downstairs and took the step stool from behind the counter. Positioning it by the front door, she climbed up and lifted the door's bell from its hook. She placed a closed sign in the window, and double checked that the door was locked. Lou would be angry to lose a morning's trade, but he would be angrier if someone woke him.

She tip-toed to the storage room, gently pulling the door closed, and set about filling more bottles with river water. She held one up to the light, and watched the flakes of dirt and lumps of muck settle to the bottom.

"How do you get away with it?" she said,

shaking her head.

Once her small cart was full of bottles, she pulled it across the room, wincing as the bottles rattled and clanked against one another.

She backed into the kitchen, but the cart's back wheel caught on the door frame. Maeve tugged the cart sideways to try and free it. The cart tipped onto two wheels for a moment, teetering, before dropping back down. Maeve watched as three bottles toppled onto the floor. They smashed, covering the tiled floor in river water and shards of glass.

Maeve held her breath, and listened to the silence.

"Please, please, please," she whispered.

"God-bloody-dammit!" bellowed Uncle Lou.

She heard his footsteps on the top staircase, tracked them across the landing above her, and listened as he slipped down the stairs to the hall.

Maeve sprinted towards the shop, passing the stairs just as Lou was regaining his feet. She threw herself through the open door into the shop, kicking it closed behind her. It bounced off Lou's toes and swung open again.

"Get back here, you bitch!" he roared.

Maeve scrambled across the floor, and reached up, fumbling for the door catch. Her head snapped back as Lou grabbed hold of her plaits and yanked them hard.

"Where the hell do you think you're going?" He pulled her plaits again, and she fell back from the door. "Come here!"

Maeve clamped her hands to her throbbing head as Lou dragged her through to the kitchen.

Glass crunched under Lou's thick socks, and shredded Maeve's bare feet. Blood smeared across the floor. Lou lifted her onto a chair, and swept the table clear of its usual clutter.

"Sit there," he said. He pulled a kitchen drawer open and dug through its contents. He pulled out a ball of string.

"Uncle Lou, I'm sorry," Maeve said, cowering as he approached.

He stopped, and pressed the back of his hand against his forehead. "I have such a headache. Bang, bang, bang, bang, bang. And you—" He gestured at the bottles and groaned; his sentence finished with a guttural expression of displeasure.

He stepped behind Maeve, and pulled her shoulders against the back of the chair. He took hold of her plaits and pulled them down, forcing her to tilt her head back. She stared at the stains on the ceiling as he tied her plaits to the chair. Tears ran over her hot cheeks. She screwed her eyes shut to contain them, knowing they would only fuel his cruelty.

She heard him step away, and the clink of bottles. He walked back to her slowly, purposefully igniting her terror.

She heard the gentle squeak-pop as a cork was removed, and she opened her eyes to see the dimpled base of a bottle above her.

Lou moved his mouth to her ear, his breath stale with beer. "You need to take your medicine."

She could hear the smile in his voice. "It will make you all better."

He grabbed her face, squeezing her cheeks, forcing her mouth open. He turned the bottle over, and its stinking contents sloshed over Maeve's face. The neck of the bottle hit her teeth hard as Lou forced it in.

The river water filled her mouth; cold and sour. Her stomach automatically urged, bubbling up. Maeve swallowed hard, the water burning into her throat.

Lou pushed the bottle down harder, its widening neck forcing Maeve's mouth open further. Somewhere beneath the fetid taste of the water, Maeve tasted blood.

Lou pulled the bottle from her mouth and placed it down with a thud. He tapped Maeve's forehead.

"Better try not to be sick," he said. "You'll choke to death if you do."

Maeve held back her tears until Lou had left the room. She heard him open the shop, greeting customers with a bright and lively voice. She stared at the ceiling, as pain crept from her neck, to her shoulders, and down her back. She counted stains, mapped out the cracks, and all the time, she planned.

8

Gretta helped Maeve onto a stool in the kitchen behind the bakery, and gently washed her face with a warm cloth. She washed her arms, and her legs. She pulled Maeve's dress, stiff with sick, off over her head, and dropped it onto the floor.

"We'll just throw that out. No point in washing it. I'll find you a dress of Topley's to wear. I keep buying them, and she keeps refusing to wear them."

She handed Maeve a soft, clean towel, allowing her to cover herself before handing over her underwear. The stained items joined the dress on the floor.

Maeve allowed Gretta to lead her upstairs to the bathroom, where the air was thick with steam and the dusky scent of lavender. Gretta helped her into the bath, and she eased herself down into the hot water.

She rested her aching head on the cool porcelain of the tub, and closed her eyes. Gretta slowly unplaited Maeve's hair, gently teasing out tangles with her fingers.

"Would you like something to eat?" Gretta asked. "Or a hot chocolate perhaps?"

Maeve's stomach churned at the thought, and she shook her head quickly.

"No. Maybe just warm water with some lemon then. It will help settle your stomach." She patted Maeve's shoulder as she stood up. "You just relax, no one's going to disturb you."

Maeve sunk deeper into the water. It soothed her muscles, and eased the throbbing in her head. She glanced up at the open bolt on the door.

Too many times, Uncle Lou had disturbed her while she bathed. Sometimes he was too drunk to even notice her there as he pissed. Other times he noticed her too much. She had taken to having very quick, cold baths, as infrequently as she could.

But now, she allowed herself to relax, and closed her eyes. She hadn't realised how tired she was, and surrendered herself to dozing.

She woke to Gretta gently shaking her.

"I'm sorry to wake you, darling, but I don't want you catching a cold in there."

She helped Maeve out of the bath, and wrapped her in a towel. She smoothed down Maeve's wet hair.

"Shall we cut this for you? It will be much easier to manage."

Maeve nodded, and Gretta helped her back down to the kitchen.

Maeve watched her hair drop to the floor like autumn leaves. She knew it wouldn't stop her uncle's violence, but it gave him one less method of torture.

Gretta chatted as she cut. "It's amazing how a bath can take away our troubles. As the knots flow out of our joints and muscles, they flow out of our heart and soul. Don't you feel lighter already?" She smoothed down Maeve's hair. "All done. There's a mirror in the hall if you want to have a look."

Hitching her towel up under her arms, Maeve shuffled into the hall. She barely recognised herself. Gretta had cut her waist-long hair almost to her jaw. It looked thicker, fuller, and curved delicately around her face.

"I look so grown up," Maeve said.

"You're almost a woman," Gretta said. "It's time you found your own way in life."

"He'll never let me go."

"Once you're eighteen, he can't stop you."

"And where would I go?"

Gretta placed her hands on Maeve's shoulders and caught her eye in the mirror. "I suppose the bakery next door wouldn't be far enough away."

Maeve shook her head.

"There must be somewhere. A refuge. A shelter."

Maeve turned around. "Maybe one hundred years ago. Back when women didn't have to endure violent men. Besides, this thing won't help me once they try to scan it." She held up her left wrist, displaying the black strip tattooed into her skin.

They both knew what it signified. Further up the cliff, every girl received her ID strip implant at birth. They were part of the system, they were tracked and traced by it. They were owned by the authorities, but they were also under its protection. Slum girls were left to fend for themselves. While a tattoo, designed to look like an ID strip, gave them freedom to move around Falside, and helped them blend in, it was just an illusion. As soon as their wrist was scanned, they would be shown for what they were: nothing but a slum girl.

"Our duty is our purpose. Our role is our life. Obedience is our freedom." Maeve whispered the administration's motto.

"Well, just you remember that you're always welcome here, and we'll do whatever we can to protect you. Why don't you go and show Topley your new hair?"

That evening, Maeve watched Lou take his usual route down to The Slip from Topley's bedroom window. They knelt, side by side, on Topley's bed and watched his figure stumble along the wooden walkways.

When he'd disappeared from view, Maeve lay down, lacing her fingers behind her head.

"What will he do tomorrow?" asked Topley.

"Who knows? Sometimes he takes it out on me, sometimes he just sulks. For days. Sometimes he doesn't seem to even remember anything happened. I don't know which is worse."

"Will he be angry about your hair?"

"He may not even notice. Until he goes to grab me by it."

"Well, you look gorgeous. Maybe a handsome boy will fall in love with you."

Maeve grimaced. "A slum boy? What? And become the wife of a scrapper, or worse, a dredger."

Topley made a vomiting sound. "No, something better than that."

"Maybe a man from further up then? A man from Lynstock, or even Haverhead. A banker, or a lawyer."

"No, better than that, Newstone. A real prince."

Maeve looked up at Topley. "Now you really are dreaming."

"People from further up come to your Uncle's apothecary, don't they?"

"Sometimes. It's that whole romantic notion of the slums. I don't understand how anyone could find this pile of mud romantic."

"Because we're outside of the system. We're rebels. Free. Wild."

"We spend half the year knee deep in filth."

Topley laughed. "True. But they don't see it like that. We're mysterious to them, something they don't quite understand. Plus, there are a lot more girls born down here."

Maeve sat up and leaned back against the wall. "Why do you think that is?"

Topley shrugged. "Good genes, I guess."

"I can't imagine that's true. It's amazing up there. Everyone's so beautiful."

"I've never been."

"You've never been up the stairs?"

Topley pulled back her sleeve to reveal her blank wrist. "I've never got the tattoo. And you can't blend in up there without it. Mum always said that their lives were none of my business, and I had no reason to venture up there. Apparently I clambered up when I was about four. An officer found me, and Mum had quite a fight to get me back. So, yeah, I'm kind of forbidden. Besides, The Floor has everything I need, I suppose."

"But there's things up there you can't even imagine. Smells, sounds, tastes. They have this stuff called marshmallow, and it's like, like, it's like kissing with tongues."

They both howled with laughter.

"When have you ever done that?" snorted Topley.

Maeve shook her head. "I've seen it though. The prostitutes do it."

"Well that's not a great endorsement."

"Maybe your mum would let you go up now. You're nineteen, she can't really stop you."

"My life is here. It's my duty to obey her."

Maeve dropped back onto the bed. "God, I wish I was a boy. Life would be so much easier."

Topley lay down next to her. "We'd just have different duties. I don't think it's really any better."

"At least I'd be able to fight back."

Topley's green eyes shone in the semi-darkness. "There's always a way to fight back."

9

The shouting outside woke Maeve. Topley was already awake, kneeling up and peering out of the window.

"What is it?" asked Maeve. She rubbed her eyes, trying to bring her mind back to reality.

"Your uncle's here."

Maeve leapt off the bed. "Shit. I need to go." She pulled her new hand-me-down dress over her head.

"Don't. Dad'll sort it out." Topley reached out to grab Maeve's arm, but recoiled from the already bruised skin. "Just... don't go back there."

Maeve rubbed her arm. "He'll kill me if I don't."

"He'll kill you if you do."

"It's not that simple."

Topley took hold of Maeve's hands and pulled her back onto the bed. "I'll hide you here. Tell him that you've run away."

Maeve snorted. "He'd probably sniff me out."

"Then we'll both run away."

"When you've never even been up the stairs? How far do you really think we'd get?"

Topley rubbed her wrist. "Then let's fix that."

The tattoo shop was in a small shack at the far end of Hole Street. Several young men lounged around outside, drinking, smoking, gambling. As Maeve and Topley approached, they straightened up, and began to show off their tattoos to one another. They flexed their muscles, and sucked in their stomachs. By the time the girls ducked through the doorway, they ached from laughing.

The interior was packed with more smoking men. In the far corner, a small curtain half-covered a doorway. They could hear the metallic buzz of the tattoo machine beyond.

A small woman wearing over-sized glasses emerged from the mass of male bodies. She smiled quickly at Maeve and Topley, before turning her attention back to the crowd of increasing testosterone.

"Out," she ordered. For someone so short, she commanded an impressive air of authority. After a second, the men filed out onto the street.

She turned back to the girls. "They're harmless, but I'm not having them annoy our customers." She sniffed as she pushed her glasses back up her nose. "Show me, show me." She held out her hand.

Topley glanced at Maeve before extending her left arm, to expose her inner wrist.

The woman examined it, tutted, nodded, and pushed it away. "No problem. He's just finishing off, and he'll be with you in no time at all. Cash or credits?"

"I have cash," Topley said.

"Sit." The woman gestured to a small bench behind them.

As they sat down, the uneven legs swayed, and they grabbed each other to stay upright.

"Is this going to hurt?" asked Topley.

"Yes. But it's not for long. And while it heals, it itches like crazy." Maeve instinctively scratched her own tattoo. "But it's bearable."

"Why am I doing this then?"

Maeve slipped her hand into Topley's. "Because it will be fun."

"I cannot believe you let me get tattooed by a guy with half his fingers missing." Topley dropped onto her bed and gently blew on her wrist.

"And half his teeth," said Maeve.

"This won't stop bleeding."

"It will after a while. Just wash it."

"And my skin's bright red. Won't they take one look at it and know what it is?"

"Well, I'm not planning on getting that close to any officers." Maeve grinned. "Plus, you're going to have to wear a dress."

Topley sighed. "I was afraid you might say that."

"When in Rome."

"Pick one out for me, I'll be in the bathroom washing this. Or throwing up. If I'm not back in thirty minutes, come and revive me."

Maeve pulled Topley's wardrobe open. "You'll

live."

In one half of the wardrobe hung a line of dresses. They were neatly pressed, and ordered by colour. It was obvious that they'd never been worn. The other half was sectioned into cubbyholes where trousers, jumpers, and t-shirts had been haphazardly stacked. In the bottom of the wardrobe was a pair of trainers, and two pairs of chunky sandals. They would have to suffice.

Maeve browsed through the dresses, rejecting the floral and frilled ones. She opted for a plain, teal dress, and a thin, black cardigan.

When Maeve had first cleared out Lou's storage room, she had discovered a stack of old fashion magazines. The pages had become yellow and brittle, but most of the pictures were still visible. Women in trousers, shorts, tops that showed their stomachs. It had been a long time since women had dressed like that.

As the female population had diminished, they had turned to the state for protection from a desperate male populace. That protection came with conditions, and as their duties and roles became more rigid, as their freedom became more restricted, so did their behaviour, and their dress code.

Maeve had hidden the magazines under her bed. Not because she pined for the world as it was, she had never known a world like that. But because she needed to know that maybe, someday, it could be like that again. Topley had fuelled that hope in her, with her cropped hair and jeans. The hope that women could be free to choose.

Topley wandered back into the room, gently dabbing her wet wrist with a towel. "I think it's stopped. What am I wearing then?"

Maeve handed her the dress, and Topley scowled at it. She changed quickly, and dipped into an exaggerated curtsey.

"You look beautiful," Maeve said, fighting back a giggle.

"This better be worth it."

Hand in hand, the girls ran down the stairs, through the bakery, and out onto the street below.

"Mum and Dad are going to ask what I was doing in a dress," Topley said as they slowed.

"They'll be too overjoyed to question it." Maeve laughed. "Come on."

They dodged their way down the busy street, skipping between the wooden walkways. When they reached the bottom of the stairs, they stopped.

The stairs were carved straight into the rock, in places there was space for three people to walk abreast, in others, it was single file only. There were places where the rock overhung the steps, and people were forced to stoop. The uneven steps had been roughly carved by hand, and the millions of feet using them had worn them unevenly smooth. Some tilted towards the cliff, others towards the drop. Many were hollowed out, like basins, where the rainwater collected to go stagnant. Several people had fallen to their deaths from these steps, commonly from trying to push their way through, foolishly thinking that their journey was more important than anyone else's. An ingrained knowledge of Falside's social order was necessary to survive the climb.

The steps were deep, and the climb was hard in a long skirt. By the time they reached the top, Maeve's breathing was ragged, and she could hear Topley breathing hard behind her.

"Alright?" Maeve asked.

Topley nodded, catching her breath. "A bit light-headed."

"You need to get your blood sugar levels up." Maeve pulled a bundle of credits from her pocket. "A lot of Uncle Lou's customers pay him with credits, but he doesn't put them through the books. He uses them to pay for his extracurricular activities down at The Slip. So he never knows exactly how many he has." She shrugged. "Want to see the screen?"

"Why not?"

Maeve led Topley up The Downs, around to Inlet Road, and into the expanse of The Hide.

The large square was bright and busy, but it had that casual air, as if everyone were on holiday. No one was hurrying, or shouting. People lounged at tables outside cafés, they gathered on benches to chat, they strolled, slowly, past the central fountain. No one here had anywhere they needed to be.

The gender disparity was obvious. Despite The Hope housing only Falside's single women, they were greatly outnumbered by men. Men came here to look over the women. To choose one. Like cattle.

The ferocity of their stares was almost physical, and Maeve felt their gaze like hands. Topley seemed oblivious to the uninvited attention, as she gawked at the screen.

Attached to the front of the buildings on the eastern side of the square, it was three storeys high, tilted towards the people below. It had always made Maeve a little nervous; she couldn't help but imagine it coming loose from its brackets, and crushing the people beneath it.

Most of the time it played advertisements, carefully chosen by the administration to remind the women of their duty to Falside. But once a month, everyone gathered here for the announcement of the wedding banns. This was the first time the bride would learn of her impending matrimony. The fountain had been installed specifically to revive women who fainted at the news.

Today it announced the birth of a baby girl; a rare event. A couple from Haverhead grinned at the camera, cradling their baby wrapped in a bright pink blanket. Another image showed them drinking champagne. It was the only time women were allowed to drink, for fear it might affect their fertility. Broad smiles to disguise their empty eyes. A manufactured image of a family who had fulfilled their ultimate duty.

And constantly reeling across the bottom of the screen, the administration's motto: 'Our duty is our purpose. Our role is our life. Obedience is our freedom.' As if anyone could forget it.

"Do you ever wish you had been born up

here?" Topley asked, still staring at the screen.

"And spend my days with a baby under one arm, and a mixing bowl under the other? No thank you."

Topley turned to Maeve. "Don't you want a family?"

"Maybe. One day. But I don't want that decided for me."

"What credits have you got?"

Maeve pulled the bundle out again, and they sorted through them. The credits were the only currency women could use, and they could only be used for their specified purpose. At least, if you were visiting legitimate businesses that is.

"A few for groceries, some refreshments, so we can get some coffee while we're here. Oh!" She shook one of the credits at Topley. "We have a luxury."

Women on The Hope were allocated one luxury credit a month. The further up the cliff you lived, the more you were allowed. But The Hope was full of luxury shops; those selling sweets and fancy cakes, jewellers, hat shops, fancy soaps and toiletries. It was another way the administration reminded them what they could have, if they played their part.

"What are we going to spend it on?" asked Topley.

Maeve tilted her nose upwards, and put on a snooty expression. "We shall discuss it over coffee."

They lounged on the fancy metal chairs, their

coffees balanced on the flamboyant swirls of the table top. A white parasol diluted the sunshine, and allowed them to sit for some time, watching the day pass by.

They chatted, as best friends do, of everything and nothing.

Maeve stiffened, her eyes searching the square. Something wasn't right. Looking towards Inlet Road, she spotted a group of officers. They moved through the crowd slowly, speaking to people, following their directions. Fingers were pointed, and the officers moved further into the square.

"I think it's time to go," Maeve said, pushing her chair backwards. "Come on."

Topley took a final gulp of her coffee, and followed closely, one hand gripping the back of Maeve's dress.

"Hurry up," Maeve hissed. "And don't turn around. Just keep moving." She quickened her pace, and pulled Topley into the alley beside the monastery. They pushed past the crates and boxes, finally breaking into The Downs at a run.

Maeve's face crushed against the man's chest, her breath leaving her with a groan. She fell backwards, her long skirt wrapping around her feet and tumbling her to the ground. She closed her eyes to give her brain a chance to remember which way was up.

When she opened them again, the monk was holding his hand out to her.

"I'm so sorry," he said. "Are you alright?"

"I'm fine. It was my fault. We were running." She looked up into his grey eyes.

His eyes widened, and his mouth fell open as he stammered, failing to get any proper words out.

Maeve took his hand, and allowed him to pull her up. He stared at her. Maeve had to tug her hand free.

"No harm done," she said hesitantly.

"Sure, sure," he replied, his brow furrowed.

Maeve huddled against Topley as they hurried away. She glanced over her shoulder.

"He's still staring."

"Let's get home."

Maeve looked back again as they reached the steps, locking eyes with the monk once again.

Topley tugged on her arm. "Come on."

10

"I hope you enjoyed your little holiday," Lou said. He strolled into the storage room and stood over Maeve, watching her work. "You won't get another one. You're lucky I'm so kind-hearted. And what's this?" He flicked her hair. "You look ugly."

Maeve ignored him.

"Not speaking?" He kicked her in the thigh. "I hope it's not a sore throat, wouldn't want you to get sick and die."

He kicked her again, and Maeve bit her lip, determined not to look up at him.

He bent down to her. "Maybe you need some more medicine."

Maeve stood up and looked Lou in the eye.

"I need more bottles," she said. She pushed past him, fighting the urge to look back as she left.

With her jaw set, Maeve strode along The Wall, not moving out of the way for anyone. Instead of turning down towards The Squeeze, where empty bottles were in easy supply, she hitched her skirt and set off up the stairs to The Hope.

Eye Street was a dark and barren place. It

cowered under the shadow of the high walls surrounding The Compound; the administration's watchtower on The Hope. Most of the houses were empty, and all of the shops were boarded up. Except one.

At the far end of the street, squeezed up against the rising cliff, was The Paper Duchess. Once a lively bar, it was now a rarely visited book shop.

Maeve pushed the heavy door open, and stepped into the dim interior. The Paper Duchess was full of dust, and the grubby windows filtered the sunlight to a filthy grey. The large, pillared room may have been grand once upon a time, but it now looked like the contents of every book shop throughout history had been tipped into it. Maeve couldn't imagine finding what she wanted in the mess. She turned to leave.

"Can I help you?" a voice said.

Maeve looked around for the speaker, but all she saw was more piles of books.

"I'm sorry," the voice said. "Stay where you are, I'll come to you."

There was a scrabbling noise, and a small avalanche of books falling somewhere. Then the speaker appeared, climbing over a pile of books on all fours. He was a young man, tall and thin, his skin was dark, and his features were sharp and distinctive. Even though he looked like a teenager who hadn't quite got used to his fully-grown body yet, there was something very attractive about him. Even more so when his face stretched into an awkward smile.

He slid down the pile to the floor with his arms wheeling. He righted himself and bowed slightly.

"Hello, madam, and welcome to The Paper Duchess." He spread his arms wide, and Maeve almost expected to hear a fanfare playing. Clearly, he heard one in his own head.

"I came looking for a book, but I'm not sure you'll be able to find it."

"Don't let the appearance of this place deceive you. This entire shop is carefully catalogued." He tapped his temple. "I can lay my hands on any book you want."

"I'm looking for something on plants. Herbs. Medicinal plants."

"Medicinal plants." He drew the words out as he thought for a moment. "Wait right here." He disappeared behind a precarious tower of books. "What exactly were you wanting to cure?" he called.

Maeve rose onto her toes, craning her neck to spot him. "Well, I wasn't really looking to cure anything. More cause something."

"Aha, I see." His voice was further away now. "Cause what exactly? Diarrhoea? Sickness? Or was it more hallucinations and visions?"

"Actually, death," Maeve called out.

There was no reply.

"Hello?"

Maeve stepped towards a mound of books, peering in behind it. She jumped as he spoke right behind her.

"And what would a nice girl like you want with a

book on poisons?" He had a small book in his hand.

"Just curious really. I wouldn't want to accidentally poison someone."

"Perhaps a simple cookbook would be more appropriate."

"Well, it's best to be sure."

Maeve reached out for the book, but he folded his arms, slipping it out of sight.

"And what would you be willing to pay for such a book?" he asked. "There are no credits for books. We wouldn't want you women getting dangerous ideas."

Maeve slipped her hand into her pocket. "I have a luxury credit."

He held out his hand. Maeve pulled out her bundle of credits and leafed through them. She pulled out the luxury one and placed it in his palm.

He looked at it, and back up at her. "And what do you suppose would happen to me if the administration knew that I sold a book about poisonous plants to a girl from The Floor? And that I took a luxury credit as payment. A credit issued in Haverhead. How exactly does a slum girl come across such a thing?"

Maeve took a step back towards the door. "Maybe a cookbook would be more appropriate after all." She took another step back. If he reported her, she'd be arrested. Maybe even killed.

He broke into a smile, stepping forward to catch her arm. "I'm sorry, I'm joking, really. Come on, I'll sell you the book." His smile faltered. "But if anyone ever asks, it didn't come from me."

Maeve nodded. "Sure."

He handed her the book. "And if you ever need anything else, maybe on torture techniques, or how to commit the perfect murder, just come back to The Paper Duchess, and Denver will sort you out." He leaned forward, lowering his voice. "That's me by the way."

"Sure." Maeve slipped the small book into her pocket and stepped back, glancing around to locate the door.

"Hey, really, I'm sorry about all that. I read too many spy novels, and fancy myself as something I'm not." He grinned again. "Really, you're safe here."

"Thanks for the book." Maeve backed to the door, pulled it open, and scurried away.

11

Kerise dropped from the rafters, landing on the floor without a sound. She reached out and clamped her hand onto Denver's shoulder.

He spun around, clutching his heart. "Don't do that!"

Kerise glanced at the door. "Was that her?"

Denver nodded. "That was her."

12

Hemlock had been easy enough to find. It grew plentifully among the tall grasses at the far end of The Floor, and its red-spattered stems were distinctive. Maeve had been careful to keep it separate from the other plants, which would be destined for the medicine bottles.

She put the basket of cuttings on the kitchen floor, and pulled out the hemlock, constantly reminding herself not to touch her face before washing her hands. She removed the leaves, and wrapped the stems and clusters of white flowers into an old towel. According to the book, the leaves would do the job.

Crossing to the sink, she scrubbed her hands until they were red. She grabbed a loaf from the worktop, took some old sliced ham from the fridge, and pulled out the small jar of mustard she'd bought on The Hope. The book said hemlock tasted foul, and she hoped the mustard would be enough to disguise its flavour.

Maeve carried everything to the table. She spread the bread with generous amounts of mustard, wincing at the smell. She layered in two slices of ham, and then looked at the hemlock. Could she really do this?

Lou strode into the kitchen and peered at the half-made sandwich.

"I made you lunch," Maeve said, as casually as she could manage.

Lou raised an eyebrow. "Lunch?" He folded his arms. "When do you ever make me lunch? It's not poisoned, is it?" He laughed at his own joke.

Maeve's heart beat like a drum. She was sure he'd hear it.

"It's a peace offering," she said quickly, stepping away from him. "An apology."

"That mustard stinks. And what's that?" He pointed at the hemlock leaves.

"Parsley," Maeve said with a smile.

Lou snorted. He grabbed the mustard-covered knife, and swept the leaves onto the floor.

"Rabbit food," he said. He closed the sandwich and walked back to the shop.

Maeve looked down at the scattered hemlock leaves. Several of them had dropped into the basket with the other cuttings. She knelt down, scooping up the leaves from the floor. Then she set about inspecting each and every cutting, removing anything that looked even remotely like hemlock. But without their distinctive stalks, it wasn't a simple task.

When she'd finished, she wrapped the leaves with the rest of the hemlock and stashed it in the storage room. Maybe, if she found the courage, she'd try again.

13

Maeve woke as Uncle Lou wrenched her thin mattress onto the floor. She rolled onto the floorboards, her nightdress hitching up to her hips.

He placed his boot on her arm, and looked down at her.

"The shop is only half stocked. Why are you sleeping?"

"We're low on water."

"Then I'll go and get some more."

"You can't. It's dredging day. You have to let the river settle first."

He pressed his boot down harder. "I know that. But there's flu going around on Lynstock. I need a full shop."

"There's just not much we can do until the river settles. You'll kill everyone if you use that water."

Lou removed his boot, and crouched down. He placed a finger on Maeve's knee and ran it up her thigh. "Well, if we can't open the shop, I'll have to find another way to occupy my time."

"I'll finish up with the water I've got. I'll use small bottles."

"Just make sure they're cheap bottles. The Lynstock lot are cheapskates."

He roamed his eyes over Maeve's bare legs before standing, and sauntering out of the room.

Maeve quickly dressed and hurried downstairs. Lou was in the storage room, peering critically into the barrel of water.

"I'll eke it out," Maeve said.

"Looks like you're low on bottles and cuttings too."

"I'll get some."

"I want that shop fully stocked by lunchtime."

"Of course." Maeve grabbed her cardigan from a hook in the kitchen, and pushed her hands into its deep pockets.

She stumbled across the mud that had baked hard into ridges and trenches, and stepped onto the wooden planks. The Wall was almost empty today. Almost everyone on The Floor was down at the riverbank, waiting, in hope, for treasures to be unearthed by the dredgers.

"Maeve!"

Maeve looked up to see Topley perched on the railings outside the bakery. She dismounted and hurried down the steps.

"I was just watching all the commotion at the river. I think they may have found something."

"Well, let's just hope it's not cholera."

Topley coughed, bending double to spit out phlegm.

"Are you alright?" asked Maeve. "I was just joking about the cholera."

Topley waved her hand before slowly straightening up. "It's just the stench of the dredging, it's really getting to me today."

"Six months worth of God knows what."

"Yeah, and six months between dredges is just long enough to forget how bad it is."

"But the vultures are still there, hoping to strike gold."

Topley closed her eyes for a moment, breathing deeply. "Anyway, where are you off to?"

"To find more bottles. Easy pickings when everyone's preoccupied at the river. Are you up to coming along?"

Topley nodded, but her cheeks were pale.

"We'll take it slowly then," Maeve said, offering her bent arm for Topley to link hers into.

"Have you ever been down on dredging day?" Topley asked.

"When I was a kid. I remember going with my mum a couple of times. I used to love hitching my skirt up, wading out into the water. I liked the way the mud sucked at my feet. I found an amazing brooch once, just unearthed it with my toes. But Uncle Lou pawned it years ago."

"Can I ask what happened with your mum?"

Maeve stopped and stared at the floor. "I don't even know, not really. One day a group of officers came for her. Uncle Lou was there, and he didn't do a thing. Just watched them take away his sister. He held onto me so tightly. I tried to get to her, but I couldn't do anything other than scream."

"But the administration has no authority on The

Floor."

"Technically, they do, they just don't really care. Just let us get on with it. I don't know why they wanted Mum. I used to ask Uncle Lou about it, but he'd always tell me to shut up."

"Do you think she's still alive?"

"I'm sure it's just vain hope, but something has always told me that she is. I feel like, if she died, I'd just know somehow."

Topley nodded thoughtfully.

"Let's go and find some bottles."

As they entered The Squeeze, Topley stopped again, gripping her stomach.

"Are you alright?" Maeve asked.

Topley braced herself against a wall as she bent over, vomiting into the mud. Maeve watched helplessly. Topley slowly straightened up, still gripping the wall for balance.

"I better get you home," Maeve said, taking hold of her arm.

"I'm sorry."

"Don't be. This is obviously more than just the smell."

"I'm sure it's just a bug. I just need some sleep."

Maeve attempted a smile. "Just don't take any of my Uncle Lou's bogus medicine."

The following day, the stench of the river still hung thick over The Floor. Maeve wandered downstairs, her mood darkening as she heard Lou already opening the shop. She enjoyed the mornings he slept late. They were her hours, and the only time she didn't need to be alert, or watchful.

She crept down towards the storage room, keen for him not to hear her. She glanced at the barrel, stopped, and went back for a closer look. It was full. And it absolutely reeked.

Against her instincts, Maeve walked up to the shop and stepped through the door. Lou was sat behind the counter with his arms folded across its polished surface. His head was rested on his arms, his eyes closed.

"Uncle Lou, did you get more water?"

Lou lifted his head and sneered at her. "You asked for more, and I delivered. Now you have no excuses."

"But it's dredged water."

"No. It's clean. I got it this morning. While you were still tucked up in your bed dreaming about daisies. I live to serve."

"It's definitely this morning's water? You didn't get it yesterday?"

Lou rose to his feet. "Can I say it more clearly for you?" He stepped forward and took hold of Maeve's hair in his fist. With each word, he gave it a hard tug. "Yes, it is this morning's water." He pulled her head back, forcing her to look up at him. "Are we understanding now."

"Yes, Uncle Lou."

He pushed her back into the hall. "Then get back to work."

Maeve sat on her sacking cushion and picked up a bottle. She dunked it into the water and held it up to the light. Maybe it wasn't dirtier than usual. She grabbed a plant cutting, and carefully inspected it. She couldn't risk slipping poison hemlock into the bottles.

14

Lou opened his eyes as the bell above the shop door jingled. He sat up, and smoothed down his hair. He didn't bother standing up. Not for customers from The Floor.

"Jean Louis Benedict Ricard at your service," he said, the fake French accent coming automatically. "How can I help you today?"

"Our daughter has a fever," the woman said. "I'm sure it's nothing serious, but she's a little delirious, and I'd like something to help her sleep it off."

The man she was with began browsing the shelves. Picking up the odd bottle, putting it back, picking up another. The constant chinking of the bottles grated Lou's headache, but the man was enormous, with arms like tree trunks, so he wasn't about to argue.

"Well then, I have just the thing." Lou pushed himself to his feet and wandered over to the shelves. He made a show of checking the bottles, as if they contained different things.

He chose a plain, average-sized bottle.

Nothing special. Nothing expensive.

"Credits or cash?"

The woman dug into her pockets. "Credits." Her voice cracked. It was a sign Lou knew well; the sign of a desperate mother. He played close attention to his customers' body language, the tone of their voice, the look in their eyes. Not because he cared, but because he knew desperate people would pay a higher price.

"Two luxury, or six standard."

The man shifted his weight, and for a moment, Lou thought he might have a haggler on his hands. He had neither the energy, nor the inclination to haggle. Let them name their price. But the woman handed over six credits without argument.

Lou wrapped the bottle in a paper bag and passed it to her.

"I hope she feels better soon."

"Thank you," the man said.

Lou frowned as they turned to leave. "Excuse me," he said. "Are you from the bakery just next door?"

"Yes we are," the woman replied.

15

Gretta wrung a cool cloth into the bucket by Topley's bed and laid it, gently, over her daughter's forehead. Topley groaned in her sleep, her eyelids fluttering. Gretta touched her hot cheek.

"Maeve came to see you, darling. I sent her away. Maybe you'll be well enough to see her tomorrow." Her voice cracked, and she cleared her throat.

Gretta heard Hex's heavy boots on the stairs, and quickly wiped her eyes. She turned to the door with as much of a smile as she could manage.

"How's the patient?" Hex asked.

Gretta shrugged. She didn't trust her voice not to betray her.

"Maybe a bit more medicine."

Gretta moved off the bed and let Hex take her place. He put his hands under Topley's arms and hefted her up to sitting. Her eyes flicked open, but they didn't focus. Hex poured some medicine into a small cup, and held it to Topley's mouth. She turned away, but he moved the cup, and pushed it between her lips.

"Come on sweetheart. If it tasted nice, it probably wouldn't work. Come on."

Topley relented, and swallowed the foul water.

"There, that's better. You get some rest now." Hex eased her back down in the bed. He bent forward and kissed her cheek. He looked up at Gretta.

All of Gretta's reserve had hung on convincing herself that she was worrying over nothing. But when she saw that same look in her husband's eyes, it was more than she could bear. Dropping to her knees, she finally let the tears come, her body heaving them out of her.

Hex knelt beside her, his thick arms holding her tight. But they couldn't protect her, and they couldn't protect Topley. Not this time.

"She'll pull through," Hex whispered. He lifted Gretta to her feet. "Come on. Lets leave her to rest. That's what she really needs."

Gretta swept back to the bed and took Topley's hand in hers. She clasped it to her chest.

"I love you darling," she said.

16

Maeve wandered out of the shop and leaned against the railings. It was three days since the dredging, and the river's stench had lost its sickening potency.

She glanced down at the bakery. Gretta had sent her away yesterday, and this morning, they hadn't even opened the shop. The thin blinds were pulled down over the window, and a small card was taped to the door.

"I hear she's sick," Lou said, appearing in the doorway.

"Who?"

"The girl next door. Your friend." He drew the word out, making fun of the concept.

Maeve frowned. "How do you know?"

"Her parents came in for some medicine yesterday. Paid over the odds too." He grinned.

Maeve pushed herself off from the railings, and ran down to the street. She raced up the bakery's steps, grabbing the door frame with both hands. The card was handwritten, and the hand that had written it had been shaking.

The bakery is closed due to a family
bereavement.
We're sorry.

Maeve felt as though her insides had dropped out of her, leaving her body cavernous and echoing. She staggered back, and gripped hold of the railing. But it was jelly in her hand, and she sank to her knees.

Crawling to the door, she leant back against it, and let the tears come. Topley was dead. The only friend she'd ever had. And she'd killed her.

Her face grew hot with anger, with guilt, and she found the strength to stand. She ran back down the steps, and into the apothecary, shoving Lou out of her way. She skidded into the storage room, and grabbed the towel with the hemlock wrapped inside.

"You idiot," she muttered.

With tears blurring her vision, Maeve ran blindly back to the street, and cut through The Cubes. She bashed into people, ignoring their shouts, and stumbled across the rutted mud. She didn't stop until the freezing water of the Falwere River was wrapping itself around her waist.

She lifted the towel above her head, and threw it, as far as she could. She rubbed at her eyes, and watched the bundle float away.

"No!" she screamed, beating the water with her fists. "I'm sorry, I'm so sorry."

She crouched down, the water running fingers

along her jawline. She lifted her feet from the bottom, bobbing in the water like a cork.

Maybe I'll let the river carry me away, she thought.

Maeve had heard stories of people trying to escape Falside by swimming downstream. There were stories of rapids and jagged rocks, bodies pulled from the water with every bone broken. There were stories of sharks, crocodiles, piranhas. Stories of soldiers on the riverbanks that shot people on sight. But the current trickled past her gently, incapable of carrying her anywhere.

Maeve stood up again. She didn't deserve an easy way out. She deserved to look at what she'd done, every day, for the rest of her life. She deserved the guilt, the self loathing. That would be her monument to Topley. A pillar of bitterness, a wreath of hatred, a banner of loneliness.

Balling her sodden skirt into her hands, Maeve waded out of the water, and dragged her feet through the mud. She didn't walk along the wooden walkways, opting instead to perilously find her way through the furrows of mud.

She stood in front of the bakery, and looked up at Topley's bedroom window. She walked slowly up the steps, her need for solace outweighing her desire to suffer. She cursed herself for being so weak willed.

The bakery door was open, but they weren't serving customers. They were packing their belongings.

Maeve stood in the doorway, water pooling

around her feet. She hung her head.

"Maeve," Gretta said. "We're leaving. There's nothing here for us anymore, and there's nothing for you either." The softness in her voice had gone, replaced by sharp corners. "You should just go home."

"I could come with you," Maeve whispered.

Gretta picked up the basket she had been packing. She looked around the shop. "That's everything. Let's go."

Gretta pushed past Maeve, with Hex following silently behind. As they descended the steps, he turned and looked back at her.

Maeve sat down on a box, a stack of rubbish was piled behind it. Maeve ran her eyes over it, looking for something familiar; a memory, a souvenir. Something that would keep Topley close to her.

And there it was. The thick, round neck of a bottle. She pulled it out and looked at it. A sprig of lavender stood inside it, and in the bottom, a thick layer of brown sludge slowly shifted. Maeve stared hard at it.

She pushed herself to her feet and ran down the steps, and up to the apothecary. She marched down to the storage room, grabbed the rim of the barrel, and toppled it, water washing over the floor. Behind it came the sludge. Thick, sickly, suffocating.

This water could have only been collected on dredging day.

And her uncle had collected it.

17

Harris knew exactly where to find Lou. They'd frequented the brothels in The Slip together for years. He knew Lou's type, and his type was cheap.

Harris gingerly made his way down the steps to The Floor. He hadn't been down here for several years, and the steps were more perilous than he remembered. At least his habit gave him right of way wherever the steps were too narrow for two people to pass.

When he reached the ground, Harris looked up The Wall. Maeve wasn't far away. It would be so easy to walk to the apothecary, and knock on the door. Physically easy, at least. Instead, he turned the other way and picked his way down to The Slip.

The girls leaned out of doorways as he approached, whistling, calling out to him. He would be a fetish to them, a story to tell, a badge of honour.

"Have you seen Louis?" he asked one girl.

"Not tonight, baby," she replied, her drunk tongue struggling over the words. "But I got something I want to confess to you."

Harris ignored her, and walked on. By the time he reached the end of the row, word had already spread.

"You can come see my Louis," one girl called out, lifting her skirt.

"I can show you heaven tonight," said another.

"Come here, I've got a sin I'd like you to look at."

Harris rolled his eyes.

"Harris."

He stopped at the sound of his name. The woman in the doorway was much older than the other girls. She was covered up, and could almost pass for a proper lady.

Harris moved closer, struggling to see her face in the approaching darkness. He frowned, searching through his memory for a name to attach to it.

"Bloody hell," he said, "is that Niblet?"

She winced. "No one calls me that anymore. It's Madam Lemaire these days." She gestured to the building behind her. "I'm a business woman now."

"Very impressive," said Harris.

Madam Lemaire picked at his habit. "No need to ask what became of you then. You were my best customer too. But maybe we can talk exclusivity deals, if you have some time. I can send all my finest girls to the monastery."

"Actually, I was looking for Louis."

She rolled her eyes. "Yeah, he's in. Want to

wait for him? We could have that conversation."

Harris sighed.

"Come on, for old times," she urged.

"Alright. I'm pretty sure I got lice from the last one I was with."

"All my girls are clean," Madam Lemaire called over her shoulder as she led him inside.

By the time Lou was brought down to the bar, Harris was drunk, with a girl lounging on either side of him. He'd lost his habit somewhere along the way, left sitting in nothing but his long underwear. The girls stroked his chest, whispered in his ears, wrapped their toes around his ankles.

He pushed himself to his feet, and the girls tumbled from him.

"Lou, at last." He clambered over tangled legs and pulled Lou into an unrequited embrace. "Get me out of here," he whispered in Lou's ear. "God knows how big a debt I've already run up."

"Where are your clothes?" Lou asked.

"Never mind them, just get me out of here."

As they staggered out, they passed Madam Lemaire. "See you soon," she said with a grin.

"You're a good businesswoman," Harris mumbled.

"You're telling me," replied Lou.

They wandered, stumbling together, along The Edge, the stinking river eager to swallow them if they fell. Lou tripped, and dropped Harris, his chin bouncing off the edge of the walkway. His inebriation dulled the pain, and Harris rolled onto his back, howling with laughter. Lou eased himself down to sit on an empty crate.

"That's going to hurt in the morning," Lou said.

Harris looked up at him. "You're right about that."

"So, how is it that Father Harris finds himself slumming it with the rest of us?"

Harris frowned. Somewhere in the fog of his brain, he remembered having a purpose. "I was looking for you."

"Why?"

Harris twisted around, managing to sit up against the shack behind him. "I can't remember." He laughed.

"It must have been important for you to come down here."

"Yes!" Harris cried with a flash of inspiration. "The girl."

"Oh."

"Yes, I saw her. In fact, we bumped into each other." Harris leaned his head back against the shack, trying to slow the spinning. "She looks just like her mother. I thought I was seeing a ghost."

"Every day I have to look into that face," Lou said. "It's like looking at my sister. Some days I'm sure there's something accusatory in her eyes, like she knows my part in it all. Every day, she's a reminder."

"How is she?"

"Like a thorn in my side."

"I was wondering if, maybe, sometime, I might come and see her."

Lou snorted. "And tell her what? 'Hi, I'm your dad, and me and your uncle sold your mum to the administration. Then we spent the money on beer and hookers.' What a touching reunion that would be."

"Maybe you're right." Harris looked down at his socks, white in the moonlight. "Where are my clothes?"

18

Maeve unloaded the filled bottles onto the kitchen table. She had cleaned up the storage room, washed out the barrel, and paid a boy to fetch her more water. Uncle Lou had no idea she knew what he'd done. That was an advantage she was keen to keep hold of.

Glancing up the corridor, she could see straight outside; the door from the hall to the shop was open, as was the front door beyond. She wandered through.

Uncle Lou was leaning on the railings, looking down the street. The air was full of shouting and screaming, with people running past to involve themselves in whatever was happening.

Maeve balled her hands into tight fists and stepped up next to Lou. Every part of her wanted to scream, to tear him apart with her bare hands. But she simply swallowed, and forced her voice into a neutral tone.

"What's going on?" she asked.

Lou pointed down the street to a tight crowd of people. "They caught some guy who raped and killed his wife. Been battering her for years apparently."

Maeve peered down the road. She could see the accused man, his face covered in blood, being dragged along. He was screaming, kicking his legs out, fighting for his life.

"What will they do to him?"

Lou shrugged. "Kill him. Maybe drown him, or just kick him to death."

"Won't the administration try him first?"

"The administration don't care about what we do. They're never going to come and investigate the death of a slum woman. It's mob justice down here. No trials, no appeals, just the death penalty. What do the administration care if another cockroach dies?"

Maeve looked back at the crowd.

"Mind the shop, I'm going to watch. You don't often get entertainment this good."

Maeve watched him clatter down the steps. Slowly, she relaxed her aching hands, and rubbed at the deep fingernail imprints in her palms.

19

Maeve settled herself onto her rag cushion, and pulled over her basket of fresh plant cuttings. She unwrapped the hemlock, and stared at it. With its clusters of small white flowers, and its feathery leaves, even its mottled stem, it looked so innocent. No one would guess what it was capable of.

She looked down at her hands. Was she capable? Able to kill indiscriminately? To take innocent lives to save her own?

She picked up her knife and chopped the hemlock down, mixing it among the other plants. If she didn't look, if she didn't know which bottles contained the lethal plant, then she wasn't choosing who would die. That was destiny's job. She may be putting the gun in its hand, but destiny would be pulling the trigger.

Maeve picked up a bottle, and held it tightly. She put it back on the pile, picked it up again.

"Here goes," she said, dunking it into the barrel of water. She listened to the bubbles fight their way from the bottle, waited for them to cease, and lifted the full bottle out. She reached behind her, and blindly grabbed a cutting from the basket. Screwing her eyes closed, she stuffed the plant into the bottle.

She opened her eyes, and inspected the medicine. No hemlock. She sighed. This wasn't going to work. Sitting the bottle on the floor, Maeve stood and wandered to the doorway. She looked back at the plant cuttings.

"I can't do this," she said.

Maeve walked up the hall, and hovered outside the door to the shop. She listened for customers; she'd been punished before for walking in while Lou was haggling a sale. She reached out and touched the handle, taking a last glance back towards the storeroom, before turning the brass globe in her hand.

She swung the door open and stepped through. Uncle Lou was stood by the window, staring at her.

"Where are you going?" he asked. "It can't be next door. Your friends there are either dead or disappeared. Guess they didn't like you very much."

"I need more plant cuttings."

Lou frowned. "You were out yesterday getting some. What are you up to?"

He moved quickly, and grabbed Maeve by the wrist. He wrenched her arm up above her head and marched her back to the storage room.

"There. What's that?" He pointed at the basket of cuttings. "Trying to sneak off somewhere? I need bottles on my shelves. I'll teach you to be so damn bone idle."

Lou lifted Maeve over to the barrel, and thrust her head down into the cold stench. Her mouth filled with it, and her stomach lurched at the horribly familiar taste.

Maeve clawed at Lou's hand on the back of her head, but he only pushed down harder.

Bubbles poured from her mouth as she filled up with the water. They slowed, and finally stopped. She felt her consciousness slip, drifting out of her body. She closed her eyes. Maybe this was the best escape after all.

Through the encroaching fogginess, she felt Uncle Lou release her, and she felt her body hit the floor. Her hip, her shoulder, her head.

Maeve woke choking on her own sick. She placed her hands on the cold stone floor, and pushed herself onto hands and knees. Her head throbbed as she retched, and her vision was dusted with spots that swarmed like flies.

The door to the storage room was shut. Maeve crawled over to it, reached up and turned the handle. It was locked. Uncle Lou had left her for dead, and simply locked the door.

I wish I had died. And stunk, and stunk, and stunk.

Kneeling up, Maeve pounded on the door. She heard Lou's footsteps shuffling across the kitchen floor.

"Uncle Lou!" she cried out.

His hand hit the door. "About time you stopped

sleeping," his voice said.

"Let me out."

"You can come out when every one of those bottles is filled. Not before. I will not have laziness in my house."

Maeve sunk to the floor. She looked at the pile of bottles. She looked at the basket of cuttings. Fuelled by hatred, she knelt on her cushion and worked fast. She picked through the basket for the hemlock, pushing the leaves into the cheapest bottles. The administration might not care what happened on The Floor, but its residents certainly looked after their own.

20

Kerise hopped up onto the narrow sideboard, curling her legs underneath her. She shifted slightly, and rolled her shoulders. She tugged at her jacket, and finally decided to remove it, depositing it on the floor.

"I don't know how you can work in here," she said.

Tale looked up from her screen. "What's wrong with it?" she asked.

"No windows, no air, that incessant hum of your computer. And it's so hot."

"That is the heat of enterprise," Tale said. "And of revolution. Come on, give me a break, I built this thing from bits begged, borrowed, and stolen. It's a bit of a dinosaur, I admit, but have some respect."

"I suppose it has its uses." Tugging an overstretched hair band from her wrist, Kerise tied back her thick, dark hair.

"Without it, we'd be searching for this article by hand. Fancy tackling those lot?" Tale gestured at a pile of storage boxes, piled haphazardly into one corner of the small room. "Be glad I digitised the back catalogue."

"Fair point."

"And you should be proud. This is the only computer The Hope has outside of The Compound."

"That you know of. There could be several underground magazines working to undermine the administration's authority."

Tale shrugged. "None as good as Asteria." She pushed her small, square glasses back up her freckled nose. She looked back at the screen, and held up her forefinger. "Hold on, hold on, here's something."

Tale's head disappeared behind the monitors. Her hand appeared, gesturing in Kerise's direction. "Just printing it out now."

Kerise jumped as the machine next to her whirred, clicked, and juddered. Bit by bit, it pushed out a sheet of paper. Kerise picked it up, snatching her hand away as if the printer might bite it.

"I hate all these machines. I always feel like they're watching me."

"These ones are harmless. We're completely off the network here, so no one can spy on us."

"Either way, I'd rather not look at a screen all day. I'd always be wondering who might be looking back. It's weird to think that just sixty-odd years ago, everyone was addicted to their electronics. Always staring at screens rather than talking face to face."

"Until the administration turned them all into microphones and video surveillance. Watching our every move."

Kerise looked at the printout in her hand. "This was the first story, when we picked up on her. Have you got the one covering her arrest?"

"Just looking for it now."

"There's a picture of her with Maeve here. She must have only been about, what, four years old?"

Tale pointed at the printer again. "Here it comes."

Kerise grabbed the warm printout and looked it over. "Oh yes, this is it. 'Selene Richards was removed at gunpoint for unspecified crimes against the state. Her six year old daughter, father unknown, was torn from her arms to be left in the care of her uncle, known as Jean Louis Benedict Ricard, the proprietor of an apothecary shop on The Wall. Selene's whereabouts have remained unknown. It is not known whether she is alive or dead.' Is there anything else on her?"

"Hold on," Tale replied. "Hmm, only one small article a couple of years later. Some woman claimed she was receiving psychic messages from Selene. But her letter was published anonymously. I mean, her name might be on the original letter, but the archives give me nothing."

"Do you think her letter is still around here somewhere?"

Tale tapped her monitor. "You could try looking through the boxes, or Denver might know. He's got a scarily accurate memory for exactly what and where everything is in this mess."

Kerise braced herself against the wall and

leaned forward. "Denver!" she screamed.

Tale winced. "Can't you *go* and get him? It is way too early to be yelling like a fishwife."

As Denver appeared in the doorway, his toothbrush protruding from his mouth, Kerise grinned smugly at Tale.

"It worked," she said. She turned to Denver. "Apparently, some woman once wrote to Asteria claiming to be receiving psychic messages from Selene Richards. Do you know if that letter's still around?"

Denver chewed on his toothbrush. "Possibly. I've got a few boxes of old Asteria letters. You prepared to dig through some dusty old boxes, Kerise?"

Kerise hopped down to the floor. "You know me, I like to know everything about a situation before I get into it."

"Never be surprised," chorused Denver and Tale in unison.

"Yes, alright," Kerise snapped. "But when I have a knife to a guy's throat, I need to know he won't have a gun against my stomach."

"I'll grab those boxes."

"I'll give you a hand." Kerise followed Denver into the corridor, and down to, if it were possible, an even smaller, more packed, less airy room. The boxes were stacked floor to ceiling, threatening to topple, and rid the planet of them both.

"Do you ever throw anything away, Denver?"

"You never know when things might come in handy." He winked as he disappeared into the maze of boxes.

"I still think we should just go and grab Maeve before she does something crazy."

"You know what we decided," Denver's voice said. "The majority ruled we wait. See what her plan is." He reappeared with a shoebox in his arms. He handed it to Kerise. "Keep your distance. You're just there to watch her."

"I know, I know. But whatever she's up to, she bought a book on poisons, so it's not going to be something good. I just want to get her out of harm's way. We can't risk losing her."

Denver disappeared behind the boxes again. "She hasn't shown any signs of having inherited Selene's abilities. We're really only still watching her out of curiosity. Is she that important?"

"Abilities or not, she's the only link to the most powerful psychic we've ever known. So, yes, she's important."

21

When Jody Kelley walked into the apothecary shop that morning, he had a bad case of diarrhoea. He bought a large bottle of medicine—it was a common occurrence, and best to be prepared for next time—and asked to use the toilet. When he was refused, he crouched under the shop's front steps to release his bowel. He had little choice about it, but it also left him with a satisfying sense of vengeance.

Stopping by his house in Hole Street to drop off the medicine, he set off to his job at The Burnt Scroll. He was the chef there, and today there was a wedding party, so he really didn't need the added complication of a toilet trip every ten minutes. Plus, he didn't want his boss finding out. Weddings meant good tips, and she'd be sure to send him home if she knew he was ill. She usually sorted her staff out with medicines from her sister. But he needed a quick-fix today.

Shortly after arriving at work, the stomach ache began. He shrugged it off as a by-product of his loose bowel, and put it down to a good sign that the foul medicine was doing its job.

But then he found himself running to the bathroom to vomit, and as he pulled the chain, Jody realised that his hand was shaking. In fact, his whole body was shaking. His legs, unable to support him any longer, gave way, and he fell to the floor, convulsing in a pool of his own shit and piss.

Luckily for Jody, he was unconscious when his lungs and heart gave up working.

Unluckily for Faith Wallace, the young barmaid, she was the next person into the toilet. As the stench of Jody's emptied bowels hit her, she vomited on the floor. Little did she know at the time, but this was the beginning of a long, and vicious spell of morning sickness that would, eventually, force her to leave her job.

In addition, the happy couple getting married that day were left with no party, and nothing to feed their guests. There was no refund given. They went their separate ways five years later, although that can't be attributed to this particular event.

Meanwhile, at the other end of The Floor, Mayra Hahn's husband had just bought her a bottle of medicine. Mayra didn't have anything wrong with her, other than an acute case of frigidity, brought on by her husband's lack of romantic tendencies. To him, a proposition of sex consisted of grabbing her crotch and winking at her. This was often done while she was otherwise engaged; cooking, cleaning, redressing after a trip to the toilet. No one could blame the poor woman for being less than willing.

But the apothecary had assured Monty Hahn that his medicine would make his wife's legs open like a well-oiled swing door.

He slipped the medicine into his poor wife's morning tea. The tea itself was foul stuff, although she insisted on drinking it on the claim that it helped her to keep her figure. Monty couldn't work out who she might be keeping it for.

He brought her tea to her in bed, and returned to the kitchen to find something for breakfast. He settled down at the enormous kitchen table—they had six children themselves, who had gone on to bless them with twenty three grandchildren so far— to enjoy his own cup of tea and the morning newspaper in peace.

After completing the crossword, Monty crept up the stairs to see if his wife had changed her rigid view on copulation. By halfway up, he could hear her gasping. Afraid that she'd started without him, he ran up the rest of the stairs so as not to miss all of the action.

Monty found her lying on the bed, her eyes and mouth wide, and her ample chest heaving. Mistaking this for an act of foreplay, albeit unusual, Monty hurriedly undressed. As he was desperately coaxing his sceptical penis into life, his wife's heart stopped.

Monty never forgave himself, and his hands only ever entered his underwear when he was emptying his bladder. Even in death, his wife managed to dissuade him from one of his favourite pastimes.

22

Harris rolled off the woman, and lay next to her, breathless. He was certainly beginning to feel his age.

The prostitute propped herself up on her elbow, her large breasts dropping to one side. She walked her fingers up Harris' chest.

"Mmmm, that was good," she said.

Harris lay back and closed his eyes. He was too set in his ways to try something new, he should always stick to what he knew he liked. He hated the sexy talk, the women who pretended they were interested, or turned on. He liked his usual women, the ones that made jokes through it, and left straight afterwards because they knew he needed to rest.

"Want to go again cutie?"

Harris winced. He especially hated the pet names.

"No can do," he replied. "I'm not as young as I used to be.

The prostitute coughed. The phlegm crackled in her throat. "I bet I can get you going again."

Harris pushed himself up to sitting with a groan. "I doubt that."

She coughed again. Harris climbed off the end of the bed. "Are you alright?"

"It's just a cough, nothing to worry about. I took something for it this morning." She coughed again. It was getting worse.

Harris backed away. "Are you sure?" He grabbed his habit off the floor and pulled it over his head.

She coughed, not even covering her mouth this time. "I'm fine, really. Don't get dressed, come back to bed. You have such a great body."

Harris laughed. "You get yourself dressed." He opened his desk drawer and pulled out some credits. He dropped them onto her stomach. "I need something to eat."

As he pulled the door closed, she started coughing again. She was absolutely hacking, almost vomiting each time. Harris shook his head.

"Better not be bloody contagious," he muttered.

Harris could still hear her coughing when he was halfway down the corridor. With a bit of luck, if he took his time, she'd be gone by the time he got back.

"Father Harris." Brother Grant stepped out of the library. "I've been thinking about what you said. About the, erm, reading lessons. For the unfortunate women."

Harris grinned. "Ready to start lessons?"

"Maybe. I mean, yes."

"I may have just the student for you. Let me get

something to eat first though. Reading lessons always make me hungry. Come on." Brother Grant trailed behind him. "What made you change your mind?"

"Someone lent me some reading material." He blushed. "Well, actually, it was mainly pictures."

Harris laughed. "Piqued your interest, huh?"

"Well, erm, I suppose so. I thought I might like to give it a try."

"Give it a try," Harris repeated. "That's as good a reason as any."

"I just had a few questions."

The dining room was already busy, and Harris queued for a bowl of what he could only describe as slop. He led Grant to the far end of a table, away from the other monks.

"What did you want to ask?"

Grant pulled a scrap of paper out of his pocket. "Will it hurt?"

"You wrote your questions down?" Harris rolled his eyes. He picked up his spoon in one hand, and rested his head on the other. "No, it won't hurt, unless you want it to."

"What?"

Harris waved his spoon. "I'm joking. No, it won't hurt."

"Will she be able to tell that I'm, you know, a virgin?"

Harris shrugged. "She'll know you're inexperienced. But don't worry about that. You own her for that hour or so, let her do all the work."

"What should I pay her?"

"Whatever you think she's worth. But don't go overboard, we don't want all the girls up here expecting big payouts."

"Should I woo her? Kiss her?"

"God no!" Harris smiled sheepishly as several heads turned in their direction. "No. Do not fall in love."

"What if I, you know, make her pregnant?"

"Then pray it's a girl, and you'll be a national hero." Harris grimaced as he shovelled the slop into his mouth.

"But will I be responsible for her?"

Harris shook his head. "Occupational hazard. She knows the risks. Blame the administration; they pushed contraceptives onto the black market, made them too expensive to buy. Besides, they can make a fortune selling their baby girls."

"If they're lucky enough to get one."

Harris pushed his bowl away. "We're the unlucky ones. The men on The Floor don't seem to have any problems in creating girls. Now, why do you think that might be?" Harris stood up.

"I don't know." Grant stood. "Diet perhaps? The air? Something in the water?"

Harris cocked his head. "Come on. If she's still hanging around, I can introduce you to your first student."

As Harris took hold of his door handle, he could still hear her inside. Rummaging through his drawers or something. She wouldn't find anything of any value, he'd had enough prostitutes in his bedroom to know better than that.

He swung the door open. She was still naked on the bed. There was vomit on the floor. She was violently convulsing, causing the bed's headboard to bang against the wall.

"Oh my God!" Grant's hands flew to his mouth. "What do we do?"

"Shut the goddamn door," Harris snapped. He grabbed the woman's legs, trying to hold her still. "Now grab her arms," he ordered.

Grant hesitated.

"Grab them," Harris said again.

Grant took hold of her flailing arms, pinning them to the bed. "We need to get help."

Harris looked him in the eye. "What we need is to pray no one heard her."

"We're not going to do anything?"

"What do you suggest? I have a convulsing, naked woman in my bed. I'm a monk."

The woman's convulsing slowed, and stopped. Her eyes flew open, looking wildly around her.

"Where is it?" she slurred. "You stole it. You stole it from me." More vomit dribbled from the corner of her mouth.

Harris stepped back, and ran his fingers through his thinning hair. "Oh God."

The woman began gasping for breath. Her eyes wheeled around, filled with panic. She clawed at her throat.

"She can't breathe," whispered Grant. He stepped towards her, his hand outstretched.

"Don't touch her," said Harris.

"She's dying."

"And do you want to risk catching whatever it is from her? I just hope it wasn't sexually transmitted."

Grant pulled his hand back.

Harris leaned against the wall. "Oh God."

She had stopped moving. Her flesh was beginning to grey.

"What are we going to do with her?" Grant asked.

Harris glanced at the window. "Go out in the garden. I'll pass her out to you. We can bury her in the graveyard."

Grant scuttled out of the door.

Harris pulled his wardrobe open and tugged out one of his spare habits. He dragged the woman up to sitting, resting her cool body on his shoulder as he tugged the habit over her head. He dropped her back down and lifted her hips to pull it down over her legs. He covered her face with the hood.

He leaned over and opened the window. "Grant?" he hissed.

Grant appeared. "I'm sorry, I didn't know which one was yours."

Harris grunted as he lifted the woman up, resting her shoulders on the window ledge. "Ready?" He heaved her hips up onto his shoulder and pushed her through the gap.

Grant made an effort to grab her, but ended up on the ground, with her body draped over him. The habit had ridden up to reveal her buttocks.

Harris leaned out of the window. "There's your first lesson."

Grant pushed her off him. "How can you joke about this?"

"Wait there, I'm coming around."

Digging the grave was hard going, far harder than either of them had expected. Once they had dug sufficiently deep that the body wouldn't be exposed by the next heavy rainstorm, Harris rolled her in.

He picked up his shovel, but Grant grabbed his wrist.

"We should say something."

Harris raised his eyebrows. "Really? The ground's consecrated, what more do you want?"

"This was someone's daughter, someone's sister. Perhaps even someone's mother."

Harris looked down at her. She couldn't have been much more than eighteen. He spoke quickly. "I commend you, my dear sister, to almighty God, and entrust you to your creator. May you return to him who formed you from the dust of the earth." He looked at Grant, who gestured for him to continue. "May he forgive you of all your sins and set you among those whom he has chosen. May you see your redeemer face to face and enjoy the vision of God forever." He looked back at Grant. "Happy?"

"It'll do. She deserved that at least."

They covered the body, and Harris stomped over the loosened earth to compress it. Grant frowned.

"What do you want from me?" Harris asked.

"A little respect."

"She was a hooker. She's probably not the only

one buried here."

Grant crouched down, tickling his fingers over the dirt. "She was the first woman I ever saw naked. And then she was the first dead body I ever saw. Ever touched. I thought that would be the most awful thing I'd ever see." He looked up at Harris, his eyes full of tears. "But to see you treat her with such dismissal. As a problem to be hidden. A dirty secret." He stood up. "I came into this position to make a difference, to do some good in the world."

Harris put his hand on Grant's shoulder. "So did I. But there's too much poison in Falside. You can't escape it."

"But I can shade others from it."

Harris shook his head. "It's too corrupt. It's too damn late for any of us." He rubbed his nose. "I'm sorry I can't give you any hope." He turned away and walked back across the garden.

23

Maeve sat on the stairs and listened to Uncle Lou haggling with a customer. She'd heard reports of a few strange deaths, but no one was near to making a connection yet. It was being put down to food poisoning, or illness. That was the trouble; everyone taking the medicine was already sick.

She stretched out her legs and leaned back, staring at the redundant ceiling rose above her. The bell in the shop chimed as the customer left.

She stood up and gently opened the door to the shop. Uncle Lou looked up at her.

"What do you want?" he snapped. The customer must have argued the price down considerably.

"Just checking stock levels. Is there anything we need?"

Lou stepped out from behind the desk and gripped her wrist, wrenching her arm above her head. "If we need anything, I'll tell you."

"You look a little short on the more expensive bottles."

Lou bent down, bringing his nose level with

hers. "I haven't seen anyone from Haverhead or Newstone in weeks. If I need anything, it's big, cheap bottles. Stop trying to be clever, it doesn't suit you at all." He thrust her arm loose.

"Big, cheap bottles it is then." Maeve rubbed her aching arm. "I'll take a wander down The Squeeze."

"Good. Maybe I can get some bloody peace."

As Maeve pulled the front door shut behind her, something hit the inside of it. Probably Lou's shoe. Now he'd be annoyed at having to retrieve it.

Maeve wandered down the steps to the street, and looked up at the bakery. It had already become a delicatessen. The sign swapped for another, the window filled with different products. As if erasing the memory of a whole life were as easy as window dressing.

Maeve wandered along The Wall and stopped at the opening to The Squeeze. She stared down the tightening alley, her hands clenched into fists. She took a few more steps, until she could see the spot where Topley had been sick. There was a bucket there now; a viciously morbid reminder. If only people knew. She wanted to grab them as they passed by, get them to stop, to look, to remove their hats and cast their eyes downward. But while Topley had been everything to Maeve, she was nothing to them.

Maeve turned back to The Wall. Among the usual current of people, the monk's black robe caught her eye. His hood was up, covering his face.

Curious, she followed at a distance. Watched

him stop outside the apothecary, watched him climb the stairs, and hesitate before pushing the door open. She heard the bell announce his arrival.

Then she heard Uncle Lou. "Get out! What the hell are you doing coming here?"

Maeve crept up the stairs, crouched past the shop window, and leaned against the door frame. The door was ajar, and she could see the monk reflected in the shelved bottles.

"I just want to see her," the monk said.

"Why? To ease your own conscience?"

"I have every right to see her. And she has a right to know who I am."

"Seventeen years ago, you decided you didn't want to be part of her life—"

"How could I have been?" the monk interjected.

"How convenient."

"As if you even care, Louis Richards. You took the girl in to save yourself from eviction. To give yourself a sob story, to act the martyr. You have never cared about her."

"At least she knows who I am."

"Don't you want to atone for what we did? Or do you not have any conscience at all?"

"We did nothing wrong!" Lou slammed his hand down on the counter. "We followed the law."

The monk stepped forward, and his reflection disappeared. "So there is some guilt in you after all."

"Maeve does not need you stirring up the past. Just let it lie."

"For whose sake?"

"You think she's going to thank you?"

"I'd like the chance to explain."

"You're an idiot. She'll hate you when she finds out what you did. What we did."

They were silent for a moment.

"Do you think she's still alive?" the monk asked.

"Just get out of here," Lou said quickly. "I don't want Maeve seeing you and asking questions."

"Just tell her I came for some medicine."

There was a shuffling of feet, a clink of bottles.

"Here," Lou said. "Take this one. With my compliments. Now get out of here, and don't you ever come back. Maeve does not need to know our part in her mother's arrest."

Maeve stepped into the doorway. "Yes she does," she said.

24

Maeve stood by the water, watching the leaves drift their way downstream. Her toes were wet, but she barely noticed. She wiped away another tear.

"I'm so sorry," Harris said. "That is not how I wanted you to find out."

Maeve rolled her eyes. "You really think that's going to mend everything? Clichés?"

"I don't know what else to say."

"Well then, neither do I."

"It's the law, Maeve."

Maeve spun around, jabbing her finger into Harris' chest. "She was Uncle Lou's sister, the mother of your child. You should have protected her, not handed her over. They don't care about us down here, they would never have known about her."

"We can't know that."

"What I do know is that I remember every second of that day. I remember Uncle Lou holding onto my shoulders, her damp hand being pulled from mine. I remember crying for weeks, and Uncle Lou beating me for it. You came here to confess to ease your guilt, he hits me to ease his own. That's what you left me to."

"I couldn't exactly take you back to the monastery."

"No. You could have done a lot more than that."

Harris took hold of Maeve's shoulder. "I just wanted you to know the truth."

"It's eleven years too late for that."

He dropped his hand to his side. "I know. But I thought Lou would care for you. I thought you'd be safe."

"You were childhood friends, right? So you knew what kind of man he was."

Harris looked out across the water, twisting his cord belt around his fingers. "Yes, I knew. He was known for getting rough with the working girls." He nodded slowly. "I knew."

"But you left me with him anyway. That man, who's taken away everyone I've ever loved."

"You're his niece. I thought, I thought that maybe you would change him."

"He's changed. Over the last eleven years he's become more violent. The longer I stay there, the closer I am to death. I can almost smell it now. He will kill me. And I fear it'll be sooner rather than later."

"Do you really think he would?"

"How many bruises do I need to show you? How many scars, or broken bones?"

Harris looked at his feet.

"Do you know how many nights I lay in the

darkness wishing my real father would turn up and rescue me? I had visions of a heroic man, walking into the shop, telling Uncle Lou he was taking me, not taking no for an answer. But instead, I got you. Full of excuses."

"Tell me what I can do."

Maeve pulled up her sleeve and held out her wrist. She pointed at her tattoo. "Make this real. Get me off The Floor."

"And swap your freedom for a life of being owned? No, Maeve. You don't know what it's like. I marry women every month, and they are terrified as they say their vows. I've known countless women commit suicide rather than marry a stranger. It's no life at all up there."

"So you just leave me with him, and wait for him to kill me? I guess that would be one problem solved."

"You're not a problem to be solved."

"No. I wasn't a problem at all until your conscience got the better of you." She rolled her head. "Did you ever worry that I'd turn out like Mum? Would you have handed me in for the money as well?"

Harris looked at the floor. "Are you like her? Can you, you know, see things?"

Maeve looked down at the large, cheap bottle of medicine by his feet. "Enjoy your medicine. Maybe that will help ease your conscience."

She pushed past him, and walked back towards The Wall. But she wasn't ready to go home yet.

25

Roscoe Cross hitched his heavy pack onto his shoulder and looked up the steps. It would be hard going with such a heavy load, and he cursed himself for letting the apothecary talk him into buying such a big bottle. Taking a deep breath, he began the climb.

Roscoe had stashed his cart in a back alley, and had been mindful enough to remove anything of value from it. Luckily, he found it just as he had left it. He shrugged his pack from his shoulder and dropped it into the makeshift cart. He pulled the top open, and peered in at the huge medicine bottle. He lifted it out and held it up to the light. It looked like nothing more than filthy water. He eased the cork free and poured some over his fingers, lifting them to his nose. It smelt like filthy water too. Still, as long as he sold it at a profit, he didn't really care what it was.

He dragged the cart out onto Hind Street, straightened his jacket, and set off for Second Stair. He relied on impulse buys, on people believing this was a one-time deal. The women on The Hope tended to hoard their precious credits, considering each and every purchase carefully. He didn't make money here.

The staircase up to Lynstock was a world away from the roughly cut steps up from The Floor. These stairs were deep and wide, edged with a marble strip, and flanked by impressive stone handrails. Beside the stairs was a slope, designed for people just like him; pedlars, merchants, delivery boys.

Roscoe took a run-up at the slope, his cart bouncing as it hit the beginning of the incline. He pushed it up, and nodded to the merchant waiting at the top.

"Good selling today," the other merchant said. "With the news about the baby girl, everyone's in high spirits. The wallets are open."

"Good to know," replied Roscoe with a smile.

Roscoe manoeuvred his cart around and set off for the bigger houses. May as well start at the top and work his way down.

He parked his cart, and kicked down the small stand. He straightened his jacket, smoothed down his hair, and knocked on the door.

The merchant hadn't been wrong. Each house he visited resulted in a sale, and he even managed to rid himself of a few items he'd been dragging around for weeks.

By the time he wheeled his cart from Buck Way into Silk Lane, it was considerably lighter, and his purse was considerably heavier.

He knocked at the first house, and waited. He

knocked again.

"Hold on!" he heard from the other side of the door.

He straightened his jacket, and practised his most apologetic smile.

The door was yanked open, and the woman behind it was red and flustered. Her hair had come unpinned, and a vomit stain patched her dress. She wiped her forehead with her forearm.

"I'm so sorry to interrupt you madam, you're obviously very busy today. But if I could just take one minute of your time to—"

"I'm not buying," she snapped. "Whatever you have, take it away."

"Really, just one minute of your time."

"You've already had it, and I don't have another one to spare." She moved to close the door, but Roscoe placed his hand on it.

"I think I may have exactly what you need here." He reached into his pack and pulled out the bottle. "This, madam, is the finest medicine from the world-famous apothecary Jean Louis Benedict Ricard. Proven to cure any sickness, pain, ailment, or affliction." He borrowed directly from Lou's usual sales patter.

The woman sneered. "He sounds foreign."

"French," Roscoe said with a perfected air of reverence. "The greatest apothecaries in the world."

There was shouting from inside the house, and the woman glanced over her shoulder. She swayed back and forth, her decision making marked in the body language Roscoe had trained himself to read.

"How much?"

"I can see you're a busy woman, but this kind of quality doesn't come cheap."

"How much?" the woman repeated.

"Fifteen credits." He listened to her intake of breath. He held up his hand. "Maybe, maybe, I can do a little better for you." He thought for a moment. "Thirteen. But I really can't go any lower."

The shouts came from inside again. Perfectly timed. "Twelve," the woman said quickly.

Roscoe thought for a moment more. "Because I can see you're busy, I will take twelve. But just for you. Don't tell your friends I went so low."

Roscoe placed the large bottle on the doorstep, and balanced a business card on top of its cork. The woman disappeared into the house, and returned with a bundle of credits. She counted twelve into Roscoe's hand. Roscoe had only paid the apothecary five.

"It was a pleasure doing business with you." Roscoe bowed. Before he came back up, the door had already been shut.

He pulled out his roll of credits, and added the extra twelve to it, snapping the elastic band back around. He slipped it into his pocket, and patted it. Today was a good day.

Roscoe sorted through the few items left in his cart. He'd need to get more supplies before continuing. In fact, he probably deserved a break. There was a small patisserie in Satin Square that sold the sweetest apricot pastries, served by an equally sweet young man.

The shortage of women had brought many men to homosexuality; the basic human need for closeness, to feel a body wrapped around them, skin on skin. It was so common—more common, in fact, than heterosexual relationships—that the distinctions, the terms, had almost completely disappeared from the language. It was almost expected.

Homosexuality amongst women, of course, was outlawed, with the threat of strict punishments to discourage it.

Roscoe sat at his usual outside table, positioning himself with a view of the counter. He didn't even know the young waiter's name, although they'd got up close and personal in the patisserie's staff toilet on more than one occasion. But today, Roscoe was in a good mood, and a quick fumble wasn't going to do it for him.

He leaned back in his chair, and slipped his hat from his head. Despite being on the quick approach to his fiftieth year, Roscoe still laid claim to a full head of thick, dark hair. His eyes had borne the brunt of his lifestyle; with heavy wrinkles from the sun, the wind, the smoking, the drinking, and the general excesses of life. But he didn't mind, and the young men didn't seem to either. He paid well, and he knew he performed well too.

The young waiter strolled over and placed Roscoe's usual coffee on the glass-topped table. Roscoe reached out, and brushed the waiter's fingers.

"When's your break?" Roscoe asked.

The waiter smiled. "Give me twenty minutes."

"But not here. I want you all afternoon."

The waiter thought for a moment. Roscoe placed his roll of credits on the table. The waiter nodded.

"I don't live far. Half an hour and I'm yours."

Roscoe leaned forward and watched the man walk away. He shifted, tugging at the crotch of his trousers.

26

The waiter's apartment was small, but it was immaculately tidy. Roscoe sat up on the bed as the waiter picked two bottles of beer from the fridge.

"What's your name?" asked Roscoe, accepting the offered drink.

"Todd."

"Do you bring many customers back here, Todd?"

Todd climbed back onto the bed and leaned back against the pillows, flexing an arm behind his head. "Not many." He put his bottle on the bedside table, and reached over, taking hold of Roscoe's hand. He lifted it to his mouth. "But you are by far the best." He slipped Roscoe's fingers into his mouth, sucking them in deep.

Roscoe reached over Todd, setting his bottle down. "Let's go again."

Roscoe woke to the sound of gasping. He opened his eyes, taking a moment to remember where he was. He looked over at Todd. He was propped up on the pillows, his eyes wide. He clawed at

Roscoe's shoulders.

"I can't move my legs!" he screamed. "I can't move my bloody legs!"

"It's just cramp." Roscoe rubbed Todd's thighs. "You just need to get the blood moving."

"I can't move them!"

Todd leaned over the bed and vomited on the floor, his whole torso heaving. "What the hell have you done to me?"

Roscoe backed off the bed, looking around wildly for some kind of inspiration. "What do I do?"

Todd pointed madly towards the door. "The alarm!"

Roscoe ran to the door. He flipped the cover up on the panic alarm and pressed it hard.

Todd's chest began to heave. "I can't feel my arms! Oh God, I'm going blind! Help me!"

Roscoe ran back to the bed, cradling Todd's head onto his knees. He stroked his wet forehead. What else could he do?

Todd's eyes grew wide as his body went into convulsions. Roscoe held him tightly, wrapping his arms around his shoulders. Todd's eyes closed and his body stilled. His chest rose and fell one last time. Roscoe bowed his head, and let the tears come. In a way, he had loved this boy.

He looked up as the door burst open and two paramedics entered the room.

Roscoe shook his head. "You're too late."

27

Roscoe tapped his fingers against the desk. They'd left him alone in the police interview room for what felt like years. There was no clock, and they'd taken his watch. It was a technique, designed to break him, to make him confess.

But he didn't know what he was meant to be confessing to. He knew that a man was dead, but it had nothing to do with him.

He chewed the skin around his thumbnail, a habit his father had beaten out of him as a child. He tugged at a loose piece of skin with his teeth, the strip tearing further down his thumb, deep enough to draw blood. He squeezed his thumb, watched the blood pool on his skin, and put it in his mouth. He could still taste the soap the police had scrubbed him with.

The door opened and the officer walked back in. Detective, inspector, something like that. The man was fat and balding, and looked like he hadn't fitted into a standard issue uniform for decades. He was chewing on something.

He sat down, and tucked his wayward tie back

under the desk. He sighed, and switched whatever was in his mouth to the other side.

"Roscoe Cross. You've got yourself in a bit of trouble, haven't you?"

"You tell me," Roscoe replied.

"One dead young man, found in your company. You don't think that's trouble?"

"Well, I'm not sure what to call it, because I have no idea what happened."

"But Todd Patton's house wasn't the only one you visited that day, was it? We've pieced together your movements."

"I'm a salesman, I visit a lot of houses. But Todd was the only one I slept with. What exactly am I accused of?"

He held up his chubby hands, a wedding ring cutting into the flesh. "Nothing, nothing. Yet. You're simply helping us with our enquiries."

"So, I'm not under arrest?"

"Not yet."

"So I can leave?"

He shook his head, and the wattle under his chin swayed back and forth. "It's not like it is in the movies. You will remain in custody until we decide if or when to charge you. And at the moment, that's looking more like a when than an if."

"What happened to Todd? What killed him?"

He took a deep breath, held it, and exhaled. "We believe Mr Patton was poisoned."

"Poisoned? With what?"

"Hemlock."

28

Harris grunted as he grabbed the pew in front of him, and pulled himself up from his knees. He rubbed blood back into his aching legs. He looked up at the carving above the altar. It looked back at him with disdain. A God warped and twisted to serve man's purpose.

There were no answers forthcoming from the half-closed wooden eyes. Harris had grown bitter and cynical over the years. All he saw was corruption, false piety, and most of it was his own. He couldn't find anything to believe in anymore.

He heard footsteps behind him, and turned around. He hurried down the aisle, and took Lacey into his arms. He eased her down onto a pew, letting her lean her weight against him.

"What happened?" Harris asked.

Lacey swallowed, her tongue sweeping over her swollen lips. "He tried to get rid of the baby his own way."

Harris held Lacey to his chest. "We'll get you sorted out. I won't let you go back to him again." At least he could save one girl.

He helped Lacey to her feet, and held onto her as she hobbled up to the chancel. They walked through the sacristy, and into the corridor beyond. Harris opened his bedroom door and helped Lacey onto the bed.

"Is anything broken?" Harris asked.

"Maybe a few ribs, I don't know."

"I'll get Father Benson to see you. But first, I'll get you something to eat. Just wait here, and rest. We'll figure everything out."

It had not been a comfortable night on the floor. Harris had borrowed extra blankets, but his joints complained as he sat up. Lacey was still asleep in his bed, her breathing heavy and regular. He watched her sleep, and knew he had to find some way to get her out of Falside.

But that wouldn't be an easy task. The entrances to the city were heavily guarded, and delivery vans were searched on both entry and exit. They wouldn't let any women leave, even if they were just slum hookers. Many women had been shot while trying to escape, and those who succeeded were on their own against the roaming gangs that would relish the opportunity to enslave them.

But there were also stories of refuges, safe houses, whole communities of women living freely. There were stories of cities where women were equal to men, where birth rates were steady, cities that weren't governed with such a heavy hand. Was the possibility worth the risk?

Harris sighed. If he could find a way out, if he could have assurances, maybe he could get Maeve out too.

There was a woman who might know. But Harris had never even seen her face. He'd spoken to her several times in the confessional, and he'd watched her walk away. Although with her long, red hair, she shouldn't be too hard to find. It was just a question of where to look.

Harris dressed quietly, and bent to gently kiss Lacey's forehead. She was warm, and stirred, emitting a gentle moan. He hoped she had found some peace in her dreams.

Harris found Brother Grant in the library, his usual stack of books surrounding him.

"Still looking for answers?" Harris asked.

"It gives me a purpose, which is more than you have," Grant replied without looking up.

Harris sat down. "I'm sorry. I know things have been awkward between us since—" He cleared his throat. "I want to put things right, pay it back. But I need you to help me."

Grant placed his pen on the table and turned to Harris. "Haven't I helped you enough?"

"There's a woman in my room. I want to help her, but I need to go and find someone who might be able to get her out of the city. Her name's Lacey, and she's very dear to me. While I'm gone, I need you to look after her. Bring her food, water, anything she wants. Talk to her. Reassure her."

"You're going to get her out of the city?"

"Yes. If I can."

29

Maeve dragged her feet up the steps to the apothecary. She hadn't been back in two days, having found unexpected hospitality in the brothels at The Slip. Madam Lemaire had fed her, and given her a warm bed. But that place was full of men with too few morals, and too many hands. It was a constant stream of Uncle Lous. And despite Madam Lemaire's promise that Maeve would only ever be a waitress, never one of the girls upstairs, she knew she couldn't stay. And there was only one other place she could go.

Maeve looked up at the sign above the door. The wooden bottle swung gently back and forth, hanging from the bracket by its cork. She'd spent most of her life in the servitude of her uncle, and she had few memories from before it.

She pushed the door open, and stepped inside.

Uncle Lou was sat behind the counter, bent over a newspaper. He looked up, and his face paled.

"You're back," he said quietly.

"You have your friend Madam Lemaire to thank for that," Maeve said. She wanted him to know it wasn't her choice to return.

"So what now?" Lou asked.

Maeve somehow hated him even more for his meekness, his embarrassment at getting caught. She certainly wasn't about to name it guilt. At least when he was lashing out at her, she could hate him from a physical, instinctual place. But to see him so pathetic, asking her for decisions, she had to actively choose to hate him.

"Just stay out of my way," Maeve said. She pulled the door to the hall open, and stepped through it. She backed up, and looked at his hunched stature.

"Actually, no, let's have this out." She took a step towards him. This man she had feared for most of her life. "How could you do it? How could you hand over your own sister? My mother. You took her away from me." She was shouting now. "How could you? Answer me!"

Maeve launched herself at Lou, punching his chest, tearing at his neck. He lifted his hand and swiftly hit her. His knuckles slammed into her cheek bone, and the impact threw her to the floor.

She rolled over and looked back at him. She recognised his expression; this was the Uncle Lou she knew.

He dropped his knees onto her arms, and she recognised the pain of her shoulder dislocating. Lou's long fingers wrapped around her neck. Maeve lay still, staring straight into his eyes.

"Do it," she croaked. "Do it!"

"I will!" He tightened his fingers. "I'll bloody kill you, and no one will even miss you, Selene!"

He let go, rolling back onto his heels. He stared at Maeve, and then down at his hands.

"Look what you made me do," he said. He rose to his feet, turned and walked into the hall. Maeve heard him stomp up the stairs.

She coughed, and swallowed down the taste of blood. She rubbed at her aching neck, and cradled her dislocated arm as she battled to sit up. She coughed again, and pain shot through her shoulder.

Bending her knees up to her chest, Maeve slowly lifted her arms to wrap around her legs, and laced her fingers together. She cried out as she leaned backwards, but her shoulder popped back into place. She gently shook it out, and struggled to her feet.

She wandered over to the counter and sat on the chair behind it. He had called her by her mother's name. Had he once had his hands around her neck?

She looked down at the newspaper.

'Death to Door Salesman: Merchant arrested for string of poison hemlock murders'.

Maeve quickly read through the first few paragraphs. They had linked a number of deaths to the merchant, even deaths from The Floor. They had the wrong man, and they wouldn't be looking for the right one. According to the families, justice had been done. There had been celebrations over his capture, protests calling for the death sentence.

That's why she'd seen bunting strung up in the slums.

Roscoe Cross. How did this man get so tangled up in this?

Maeve looked around the shop. She needed to increase production. She had to bring the finger of suspicion here, and there had to be no doubt about it.

30

Lacey had been at the monastery for three days, and Harris had failed to find the red-headed woman.

He knew Lacey was getting anxious. Her pimp would have expected her back, and it wouldn't take him too long to come looking for her. Harris kept feeding her, nursing her, sleeping on the floor. But they were both aware that this was just a reprise, an intermission. Sooner or later, Harris would need to find her a way out of the city, or she would have to go back to her pimp.

Harris couldn't let her end up dead. Not Lacey.

He glanced towards the window. Maybe there was a way. But he'd need Brother Grant's help again.

Grant wiped his forehead with his sleeve. He dug his shovel into the ground and leaned against it.

"So, a few days ago, we buried her, and now we're digging her back up?"

Harris crouched by the open grave. The smell was unbearable. He reached in and pulled back the habit's hood, turning the girl's face towards Grant.

"Does she look familiar?"

Grant took a hesitant glance, before taking a closer look. He looked away. "Alright, she looks like Lacey."

"All the girls I choose do. She's the woman I want more than anyone, and the only one I won't touch. Can't touch. She's a goddess."

"But will her pimp be fooled?"

Harris looked up at Grant. "When I've finished with her, there'll only be one way to identify her as Lacey."

Grant held up his hands and took a step back.

"It's alright," Harris said. "This is my mess. You don't have to stay for this."

He looked back down at the body. He pulled a scalpel from his pocket, and placed it beside the shallow grave. Climbing down on top of her, he positioned his thumbs on the eyelid, and began to push.

Harris found one of the old hearse carts in the back storage shed. It had a large, central pair of wheels, and a set of handles at either end. The steps down to The Floor would be hard-going, but this would be easier than carrying her.

Lacey collected herbs, flowers, and other fragrant plant cuttings from the garden, and laid them around the body to try to disguise the stench a little.

Grant walked in front, his back turned to the body. It was covered with a sheet, and laid with plants, but the stink was still terrible. Grant didn't deserve to be facing it. Harris was amazed he'd talked the novice monk into helping at all.

They stood at the top of the steps and looked down. They'd waited until dusk, so that they had fewer witnesses, but the deepness of the shadows on the uneven steps could prove fatal for them both.

"We'll just have to take it really slowly," Harris said. "Feel each step before you tread down to it. Maybe I should go first."

Grant looked at the body. "No, I'll be fine." He picked up the front of the hearse and, gingerly, stepped down the first step. He slipped down the next. "Don't push!" he snapped.

"I'm sorry," said Harris.

Grant continued, pausing before stepping down each step.

Progress was frustratingly slow, and they stopped every few steps to roll their aching shoulder joints, and stretch out their cramping hands. Harris' knuckles were already bruised and sore from beating the corpse.

"We're going to be here all night," Grant grumbled.

"I really appreciate you doing this," Harris said. "Thank you."

Grant looked out towards the river. "Despite everything, Father Harris, I still look up to you. And while you may be selfish, and weak to sin, there's a good heart inside you."

Harris nodded. "Thank you, Grant. That means

a lot."

Grant wrapped his hands around the hearse's handles. "Let's head on."

When they reached the bottom of the steps, they heaved the hearse onto one of the wooden planks.

"Which way?" Grant asked.

"Straight on, we'll take her down through The Cubes. The Slip is full of brothels and bars. It'll be busy there."

Half way down The Cubes, they ran out of walkways, and had to heave the hearse over the peaks and troughs of the mud. Harris shoved the hearse forward, and the jolt sent Grant flailing to the ground.

"Are you alright? Grant?"

The novice monk slowly rose to his knees, and then pushed up to his feet. He turned around. His habit was smeared with mud and dust from top to bottom.

Harris stifled a laugh, and emitted a tight grunt. He waved his hands at Grant. "I'm sorry," he squeaked.

Grant looked down at himself and grinned. "Camouflage," he said.

Harris let his laugh loose, grabbing his belly and howling. Grant braced himself against the hearse as he shook with laughter.

"Come on," spluttered Harris. "Just a few more feet to go."

When they reached the edge of the river, Harris dragged the body from the hearse, and positioned her, face down, in the wet mud. Her white skin shone in the moonlight, like a beacon announcing Harris' sin.

He crouched down, and pulled her damp hair back from her face.

"Thank you," he whispered. "I'm sorry for all this." He looked up at Grant. "She'll be found soon enough. Let's get out of here."

31

Harris gave a long sigh as he recognised her voice. He leaned forward, and peered through the grille that separated them.

"Forget all that, I'll pardon you everything if you help me."

The red-headed woman leaned back, hiding her face from him.

"What can I do for you Father?"

"I need to get a woman out of the city. Can you help me?"

There was a silence. "What you're speaking of is impossible, Father, and treasonous. I don't know why you would think I could help you," she said flatly.

"I promise, this isn't a trick to catch you out. Please, I'm desperate, and I don't know anyone else I can ask. Some of the things you've told me here, it gave me the impression you knew people."

She leaned forward again, but kept her eyes fixed forward. "Perhaps I do," she whispered.

"Will you come and meet her?"

The woman nodded and rose to her feet.

Harris stood, pulled back the red curtain, and stepped out of the confessional. A quick scan of the church told him it was empty.

"Follow me." He walked swiftly, and the woman followed closely behind. He checked the corridor before opening his bedroom door.

The woman swept across the room and took Lacey's hands in hers. She turned them over and inspected the tattoo on her wrist.

"A slum girl," she said. "That makes things a little easier. No scanners to pick up her movements." She stroked Lacey's hair back. "And pregnant too? Your pimp, I'll bet."

"How do you know?" Lacey asked.

The woman simply tapped her head with her forefinger.

"I'll do what I can, but you only get one shot at this. I will contact you with a time and a place. If you're not there, they will not wait for you. I will also give you a password. Without it, you won't get a ride. This could happen at any time, but you'll only get an hour or so notice, so be prepared." She looked up at Harris. "Keep her safe."

"Where will they take her?" Harris asked.

The woman shrugged. "A safe-house somewhere." She looked back at Lacey. "But after that, you're on your own. Are you ready to do this? You have a little one to care for."

"If I stay here, he will kill me. I don't have a choice."

The woman leaned forward and kissed Lacey's cheek. "None of us do." She stood and smoothed down her dress.

Harris led her back into the corridor. "Thank you, thank you so much."

"Do not tell anyone about this, or we're all dead."

"I understand. Can I get in contact with you in the future?"

She looked up at him. "No."

"Can I at least know your name?"

"No."

She walked quickly, retracing their steps back to the church. She stopped by the altar. "If you need me again, write to Asteria."

"What is that?" he called after her. But she didn't turn around.

32

Two weeks had passed and Maeve hadn't heard of any other poison cases. A prostitute had been found by the water, but she appeared to have been beaten to death. Half the shop was stocked with poison, but business had been slow, putting Uncle Lou in a particularly dark mood. Maeve opted to simply stay out of his way.

Maeve leaned on the railings outside, watching the delicatessen shutting up for the evening. Now and again, she glanced up at Topley's window. Topley had been like a sister, and Gretta and Hex like replacement parents. But now they were all gone.

She twisted her hair around her fingers. It had grown considerably since Gretta cut it. She'd be able to plait it again soon.

Maeve wandered back into the shop. She heard Uncle Lou stumbling down the stairs. He staggered across the hall and bumped into the door frame as he came into the shop. He stared at Maeve, his eyes unfocused.

Gripping hold of the shelves, he lurched to the

front door.

"Goodbye," he slurred, and waved his hand at her.

She listened to his feet clatter down the stairs outside, praying that he'd fall and break his neck.

Uncle Lou was never drunk before going out. He didn't keep alcohol at home. This was not a good sign.

Maeve was still awake when she heard Lou came home. She had been listening out for him, too scared to fall asleep. She listened to him banging about in the shop below, breaking glass. Lots of breaking glass. This was purposeful vandalism, not a drunk man stumbling about.

She crept down the stairs, and lowered herself onto a step halfway down. She could see Lou flailing his arms around the shop, his ravings largely incoherent, peppered with curse words. They were clear enough.

He appeared in the doorway, his head wheeling around, his eyes unable to focus on anything.

He waved a finger in her direction. "You!" he yelled. "You did this."

Maeve clung to the banister. "Did what?"

"You. You made me lose. You're a bad omen." He took a few steps towards the stairs, his body moving faster than his feet. "You and your crazy mother." He sat heavily on the bottom stair, and dropped his head into his hands.

Maeve couldn't make out what he muttered.

He lifted his head and looked up at her again. "I've lost everything," he said.

Maeve shifted up to the next step.

"Don't you move!" Lou slammed his hand down onto a stair. He twisted, and turned over onto all fours. "I had such bad luck tonight, that I lost every credit I had." He crept up the stairs towards her. "You are a bad omen. You and your hinky jinky genetics. You probably made me lose, you little witch."

Lou snapped out his hand and wrapped it around Maeve's leg. Maeve grabbed hold of the banister as he began to pull. She screamed, kicking out at him with her free leg. She kicked the banister, hard, forcing her big toe out sideways.

Instinctively, she brought her foot back into her body, and grabbed hold of it with both hands. Lou tugged her down the stairs. He crawled over her, pinning her down with one knee as he fumbled to unbutton his trousers.

Maeve kicked out again, clawing at his face. He loosened his hold on her, and she managed to twist over onto her stomach.

He pinned her down with his whole body, and with his mouth in her ear he whispered "I don't care which side it goes in."

Maeve grabbed hold of the banister and heaved herself out from under him, pain ripping through her shoulder. He reached out, and grabbed her thigh, his fingers driving into her flesh. He pushed up her nightie and moved up the stairs again.

She hauled herself further up and kicked out once more. This time her foot made contact with his face, and she felt his nose give. He grabbed her again, pushing his hand up between her legs.

Maeve grabbed the last rung of the banister and pulled herself away. Lou was up on his knees, rising up to grab her. Maeve kicked out, her heel slamming into his shoulder.

She watched his face change to panic as he lost his balance. He scrabbled for the banister, but he was already falling. Maeve didn't wait to watch him hit the bottom.

She hobbled across the landing and into her bedroom. She heaved her bed across the bare floor, and jammed it under the door handle. She took the blanket from it, and nested herself in the far corner of the room, her heart pounding.

Cuddling her throbbing foot, she curled as small as she could. And she wished that she could just die there.

33

Harris bustled Lacey out of the monastery. He'd considered disguising her as a monk, but had settled for some demure clothes from the charity donation box. He'd put some extra in a bag for her, along with food, water, and a fistful of credits, also from the donation box.

A little less than two hours ago, a man had entered the church and asked for Father Harris. He had said three words to him: midnight, Second Stair, Hestia. He had then turned, and walked out of the church.

Harris tugged the hood of Lacey's coat up. She bowed her head and they hurried through the darkness. They turned into Second Stair and looked up the empty street.

"Where do we need to be?" Lacey whispered. "At the actual steps, further up the street?"

"At the exit, I presume."

Falside had few roads going in or out of it. The majority of its supplies came via the river, with several slum workers receiving generous pay packets to see deliveries safely up the steps. One road cut through the cliff from Second Stair on the Hope. Another, on the other side of the city, from Haverhead. There were several routes in and out of The Head, but that level was not open to the general population. It allowed the administration to tightly control what came in, or went out of the city.

Harris had heard the stories of people attempting to escape. If they were caught, they were gunned down. Men, women, children, even babies had been killed. The law was rigid; if you tried to leave, you were committing treason, and the punishment for that was death. No exceptions.

They scuttled along the street, keeping close to the buildings where the shadows were at their darkest. Ahead of them, the road narrowed, and they could hear the low rattle of an engine idling.

"Come on," Harris whispered, and took hold of Lacey's hand.

They kept close to the buildings until the end of the row. Harris stepped forward. One man was loading boxes into the back of the old, battered truck, and Harris could see the reflection of the driver in the wing mirror.

He nodded to the man. "Hestia," he said.

For a moment the man didn't react, and Harris wondered if he had the wrong truck. But then he squinted into the darkness, and beckoned Lacey forward. Without another word he lifted her into the truck as if she were just another box. He gestured for her to move forward, towards the cab.

Harris' hand was still outstretched, and the sense of her hand in his lingered.

The man bumped against him. "You better go," he said.

Harris retreated, but he didn't go far. He wanted to see her out of the city, he wanted to know she was safe. His chest ached from the loss of her, but he had to get her to safety. Maybe this small act would redress the mistakes he'd made. With Lacey, with Selene, with Maeve.

Two more women were lifted into the truck, one little more than a child. The back doors were locked, the man climbed into the cab, and the truck lurched forward. Harris stepped into the street as he watched it rumble away. He could see the lights of the checkpoint bleeding orange into the sky.

He kept his eyes on that glow.

"I haven't been the best disciple," he whispered. "I haven't obeyed, or honoured your word. I've sinned, and I've lied, and I've let people down. But I'm ready to make up for that. And if you ever grant me anything, grant me this. Keep that truck safe. Keep Lacey and her baby safe. And I will be the greatest monk this world has ever seen." He pushed his hand into his pocket and twisted his prayer beads around his fingers. "Please."

Gunfire echoed against the cliffs, the sound bouncing around like rubber. Harris started running.

As he approached the scene, he saw the bodies of the two men lying on the ground. The three women clung to one another.

Harris raised his hands. "Please, please stop," he called out.

He felt the heat of the torches turned on him,

and watched the guns wheel around to focus on his body. Harris slowed and stopped.

"Please, I beg of you, stop."

"It's a monk," a soldier said.

"Lower your guns."

"This doesn't concern you, Father."

"Please, don't kill them. Please, no more bloodshed," Harris said.

A soldier approached, placing his gloved hand on Harris' chest. "This doesn't concern you," he said forcefully.

"I'm just asking for innocent lives to be saved."

"They are traitors to the administration."

Harris opened his mouth again, but his voice was drowned out by the gunfire. He screwed his eyes shut as he saw Lacey's body convulse from the impact.

34

While Maeve was curled up in the corner of her room, Harris was on his knees on the rocky road off Second Stair.

There was no solace for either of them.

35

Avery Aguilar was a well-respected man on The Floor. He was the dock master, responsible for ensuring any deliveries by boat were delivered, intact and untouched, to The Hope. It wasn't an easy job, but his reputation for being a fair man, while taking no bullshit, allowed him to be authoritative without attracting bitterness from his subordinates. He was also the only person on The Floor who carried an administration-issued gun.

Avery was the embodiment of professional cool-headedness while on the job, but his home life was surprisingly turbulent.

Those who knew Avery through his work would be surprised by the quick-tempered, irrational man he became when he came home and locked his front door each evening.

Avery's youngest son was nothing but a disappointment to him. On the cusp of his thirties, Willis lived in his parent's home with his wife and their constantly screaming baby.

Willis was one of those people who always claimed circumstances were against them. Any misfortune in his life was due to other people and their actions, and he never attributed it to his own poor decisions. Avery knew better.

Willis had started life well enough. He became a farmer's apprentice, learning how to raise cattle, how to milk, calve, and graze them. He was an impressive apprentice with a bright future ahead of him. Avery had been so proud, happy to support Willis however he could, even when it meant an evening of studying books on agriculture together.

The opportunity arose for Willis to purchase some grazing land, and he set his heart on it. In those days, when Willis wanted something, he put his entire soul into it. He worked hard, saved hard, and went to the land auction with, what he thought, was plenty of money to purchase the land. A bidding war ensued, and he lost out. Over the next month he spent all of the money—which could have bought him another equally suitable piece of land—on gambling, alcohol, and prostitutes.

That's how he met his wife, Lucille. He got her pregnant, and nine months later, she knocked on his door with a baby in her arms, and a very angry pimp. Avery was forced to buy the woman for his son. Of course, this baby came with no solid proof that it was actually Willis' child.

For the last few days, Lucille had been sick. She was confused, feverish, plagued with headaches. The baby had caught whatever virus it was, and its tiny body was too weak to fight it. They had buried it behind the house just last night. Desperate to save his wife, to salvage something of the life he had grown accustomed to, Willis found himself in the apothecary shop, handing money to Jean Louis Benedict Ricard.

He couldn't have said how much he parted with, he had stopped at several bars along the way. But the bottle was a pretty pale blue, with a long, slender neck, and it reminded him of Lucille. Or rather, his romanticised, intoxicated image of her.

Had he been sober enough to look, to remember his apprenticeship training, he would have instantly recognised the plant inside the bottle as poison hemlock. And had Avery not been so relieved to see the end of his unwelcome daughter-in-law, he would have checked the bottle himself.

Willis buried his wife next to his baby. Within a year, he would be dead himself, having left a gambling debt foolishly unpaid.

36

After three days, hunger drove Maeve from her bedroom. Before removing the bed from the doorway, she sat and listened intently to the house. It was silent.

She eased her bed back, creaking inch by creaking inch, until there was enough gap for her to slip through. She didn't need much room.

She stood on the landing, one hand wrapped around the door handle. Her bedroom was her life raft, and she was about to swim into unknown waters.

She crept across the floor, and stopped at the top of the stairs. She looked down them, not sure what she felt when she saw Uncle Lou wasn't still lying there. Equal parts disappointment, relief, and fear.

She listened again, but still, the house stood silent.

Maeve crept down the stairs, slowly, both feet on each step, stopping to listen each time. The door into the shop was open, and Maeve could see the glitter of broken glass covering the floor.

Wherever Lou was, he wasn't open for business.

Maeve scampered down to the kitchen. She glanced into the storage room as she passed. In the kitchen she found two apples, some bread, a jar of peaches in syrup, and half a bag of raisins. Gathering the supplies into her arms, she returned to her bedroom. She laid the provisions on her bed, and was going to climb over it back into her room when curiosity got the better of her.

It beckoned her towards the stairs up to Lou's room. It coaxed her up them, step at a time, and invited her to peer around the door frame.

Uncle Lou was lying on his bed, fully-clothed. A wine bottle had slipped from his dangling hand. His feet hung off the end of the mattress, his head was tilted back with his mouth wide open.

Maeve tip toed across the floor. She brushed his forehead with her hand. He was cold, but still too warm to be dead. She took a step back. Another. Another. She reached her hand behind her and took hold of the door frame.

"Don't go," said Uncle Lou.

After three days of silence, the sound of a voice seemed unfamiliar, and it took a moment for Maeve to decipher the words.

"You know I have to," she replied, testing her own vocals.

He turned his face to her, his swollen, crooked nose blackened with bruises. "Look at me."

"It's nothing less than you deserve."

"And what do you deserve?" He smiled, revealing a gap in his front teeth.

"Better than this."

Lou laughed a strangled, gurgling laugh. "You're a slum girl. The daughter of an illegal, unregistered psychic. Your mother was shunned by her entire community, and you will be too. Everyone knows who you are. Everyone will wonder if you have it too. You think you're so above everyone, but you are as far down the heap as it's possible to be. You're tainted, soiled. You aren't worth anything to anyone. Except, maybe, the administration. Perhaps I'll hand you in and see what they want to do with you. Cut open your brain, perhaps."

"So what if I walk straight out of the front door then?"

Lou shrugged and rolled onto his back. "And go where? Daddy doesn't want you either."

Maeve looked at the floor. She knew he was right.

"I need a doctor," Lou said. "I need someone to fix this nose you broke. And reset my fingers." He lifted up the other hand. His fingers were sticking out at awkward angles, twisted like a hawthorn tree. "Get me a doctor, or I'll hand you over to the administration."

Maeve turned and went back down to her bedroom. She sat on her bed, and watched the door while she ate. When she had finished, she went down to the shop and swept up the broken glass, and mopped up the water and sodden plant cuttings. Only then did she go to find a doctor.

The Floor had two doctors. Dr Stein had a

smart surgery on The Wall, where he proudly displayed his framed certificates. Dr Fischer lived in Hole Street, and performed surgery on his kitchen table. This was where Maeve headed.

37

While Uncle Lou recovered in bed, licking his wounds and wailing self pity, Maeve restocked the shop and greeted customers with a friendly smile.

One of those customers was Cora Larson. Cora was a self-taught, naturally talented, unregistered herbologist who had a penchant for study and research.

Among her trusted circle of friends and acquaintances, mostly introduced to her by her sister, she concocted and sold salves, pastes, scrubs, creams, and teas that, unlike Lou's medicines, had a proven track record of curing most things. Her customers were regular, loyal, and fiercely protective of her.

Curious to check out her competition, Cora browsed the shelves of the apothecary shop, and she quickly saw Lou's medicines for what they were. Unable to believe the unabashed fraud, she purchased a cheap bottle to study in more detail when she got home.

On returning to her small kitchen, she uncorked the bottle and found her suspicions to be correct. River water. She plucked the plant cutting out, and her eyes widened as she promptly dropped it.

She poured the river water down the drain, and spent the next hour scrubbing both her kitchen, and herself, until both were shining.

Jonas York had met his wife Fay when he was fifteen years old. He went home and told his parents that he had met the woman he was going to marry. They laughed, knowing how quickly passion can fade when you're young. But Jonas never looked at another girl again. They were married three years later and, although their efforts to have children never resulted in any, they were blissfully happy. Jonas worked hard, went for a regular drink after work, and returned home eager to see his wife.

Things began to go awry when Fay's mother got ill. It wasn't something that medicine would fix; something went wrong in the woman's soul. She became paranoid, agoraphobic, a severe hypochondriac. She became germ-phobic, scrubbing her hands until they bled. Jonas and Fay sold their own house and moved in with her.

One morning, Fay came downstairs to find her mother sat at the kitchen table. She had slit her wrists open and sat patiently while she bled to death.

Fay slipped into a deep state of depression, blaming herself for her mother's death. And then, she herself, began to show the same symptoms;

paranoia, agoraphobia, hypochondria. She was convinced it was genetic, and simply gave into her fate, but Jonas wasn't so fatalistic. He believed that guilt had driven her to adopt her mother's persona, in an effort to keep her alive somehow.

Jonas worked hard all day at the tannery, and went to night school to study psychiatry, determined to find a cure. He paid a girl to take care of his wife, although his heart ached at not being able to take care of her himself. He told himself to focus on the end goal, and he kept looking forward.

Fay had inherited some money from her mother, and she used it to bribe the girl to buy her medicine for a whole range of illnesses she didn't have. The girl dutifully did so, and kept this secret from Jonas.

Tonight, Jonas returned from night school as usual. He walked into his home, and made himself a strong cup of tea. And then he went upstairs to kiss his wife.

The girl wasn't by her bedside. The girl wasn't in the house.

He walked to Fay's bed, and pulled back the plastic curtains that she insisted surrounded her. There was vomit on her pillow, and the bed stank of urine. He touched her cheek, but he already knew she was dead.

That was the moment Jonas York's life lost all meaning. He climbed into bed with Fay, wrapped his arms around her cold body, and willed himself to die.

He may have, had his boss not come to find out why his most reliable employee hadn't shown up for work for two days running.

Once Jonas had some sense talked into him, and agreed for Fay's body to be removed for cremation, he found a new purpose. He would find that girl and make her suffer as Fay had.

Drunk, Jonas hammered on the girl's front door, and her confession sent him to another door. That of Jean Louis Benedict Ricard.

38

It was only Lou's second day out of bed. His face throbbed, and his right eye was still swollen half shut. His hand had been crudely strapped by some charlatan of a doctor, and Lou could tell the blood supply wasn't getting through to his third finger. He looked a mess, but he was upright.

Stumbling around the kitchen he'd found half a box of oxycodone. They were a little out of date, but Lou washed one down anyway.

He was halfway up the stairs when the hammering on the door started, slicing through his brain.

He staggered to the door, yanked back the bolt, and pulled it open. The man on the other side almost tumbled in on him. He was red-faced, his fists were clenched, and he already had a foot inside the door. This was not going to be a good morning.

Lou stepped back and switched into life-preservation mode. It was his most comfortable state when it came to confrontation. He raised his hands and shrunk back.

"You killed her!" the man was yelling. "You killed my wife!"

It was far too early in the morning for this kind of riddle.

"I don't even know your wife." Lou's pleading voice was a well practised one. He bent his knees and blocked his face with his arms, as if he expected to be hit. It worked on thugs that weren't entirely intent on hitting him.

"Your medicine, your medicine killed her! She wasn't even ill. It was all in her head." The man began slapping his hands against Lou's forearms.

Lou relaxed. The man was angry, but he was little danger. Lou straightened up and easily pushed the man away. He staggered backwards, collapsing onto the window seat. He began to sob.

"I loved her, and you took her away."

Lou sat down next to him, and slipped easily into his role as the great French mediciner. "I'm sorry for your loss, but it must have been something other than my medicines. What was wrong with your wife?"

"Nothing. It was all in her head. It was grief."

"Perhaps she just gave up."

The man looked up at him, his cheeks wet. "No. She wouldn't. You had a hand in this, and I'll see that you pay for it." He stood up, straightened his jacket, and left.

Lou shrugged. What could one crying man do?

39

Disappointed, and unsatisfied, Jonas walked to his favourite bar; The Burnt Scroll. The landlady knew him well, and he often got extra drinks on the house, or a bowl of fried potatoes from the kitchen.

He sat at his favourite table, and spread his meagre funds out in front of him.

Reva, the landlady, laid her slender hand on his shoulder. He looked up at her, and her red lips smiled. She was always glamorous; like one of the women from the old movies they showed sometimes. Back when romance was still a concept people believed in. But while Jonas could appreciate the effort that went into her manicured nails, and the rolls and curls of her hair, he had never lusted after her. Not once.

"The usual?" she asked.

He pushed a few coins around the table.

"On the house," she said. "And something to eat, you're all skin and bone."

Reva disappeared and Jonas stared at his wedding ring. He twisted it around his finger. In a few days, Fay's ashes would be delivered to him in a box. He'd sign for them, as if she were a delivery of tools, or food, and he would store her away. And what is that to show for the happy years she brought him?

Reva placed his drink in front of him. He looked up and forced a smile.

"Talk to me," she said.

"I have nothing but regrets to offer you."

"Then give me those. Maybe I can carry some for you." She placed her hand over his. It felt peculiar to have another woman touch him, but he didn't pull away.

"Why wasn't I there? Why couldn't I save her? Why did she keep secrets from me?"

"What secrets did she have?"

"The girl was buying her medicine. Medicines she didn't even need."

"I wouldn't have imagined it. I know how solid you two were."

Jonas nodded. "I think that's what killed her. I'm certain of it. But what can I do? I can't prove it."

"Tell me what happened."

"When I asked our girl she said that, within hours of drinking the medicine, she got ill. She vomited, grew delirious, convulsed. She could barely breathe at the end, and eventually, she stopped altogether. It took half an hour at most. Surely, only a potent poison could do that."

Reva tapped her finger against her chin. "I don't want to alarm you, Jonas, but that sounds very similar to how my chef died. You know, Jody. He was found in the toilets just an hour after he'd arrived for work. His bruised hands and knees suggested that he'd been convulsing in there. And there were—" she cleared her throat "—bodily fluids everywhere. Maybe I should ask my sister. She might have some insight."

40

Harris didn't lift his head when he heard someone approach, nor when the pew creaked as they sat down. He already knew who it was.

"Are you going to speak to me today?" asked Brother Grant.

Harris didn't reply.

"Come on, you've barely moved for days now. What are you praying about?"

Harris slowly lifted his head and unclasped his aching hands. "I'm praying for a sign that there is anyone there to pray to."

"And how's that going?"

"So far, I've been met with silence."

"Now you know how I feel." Grant smiled weakly.

Harris bent his head and closed his eyes again. He felt Grant's hand rest on his shoulder.

"I'm worried about you."

"Because I'm losing my faith?" Harris mumbled into his chest.

"I don't care about your relationship with God. I care about your relationship with the people around you. Because that's what you're best at, Harris, engaging people on their own level. That may be God working through you, or it may simply be the way you are, either way, the world needs you."

Harris lifted his head again. "Does it shit. I couldn't save one of the desperate women out there, not even one. I abandoned my own daughter to the care of a violent, heartless man, and sent her mother to, most likely, her death at the hands of the administration. The world doesn't need that kind of help."

"But that's all things you can set right and make up for."

"Really? Maeve doesn't want to know me, and Lacey is dead. How do I fix any of that? I should have just stayed out of both their lives."

Grant stood. "At least come and have something to eat. It'll make you feel better."

Harris shook his head. "I don't deserve to."

"Don't say that. You're far more use to us alive. Think of the reading programme." Grant smirked, before breaking into a giggle.

Harris couldn't help but smile.

"There you go," Grant said. "Things don't have to be all that bleak."

Harris allowed Grant to pull him to his feet. "What would you do?"

Grant patted him on the shoulder. "I wouldn't give up on any of them."

41

Kerise dropped from the flat roof, and stepped in behind some bins. She ducked down as the front door of the house opened. A woman stepped out, and tossed potato peelings onto the garden. She wiped her hands on her apron and looked up at the emerging stars. She sighed deeply.

Keeping low, Kerise moved out from behind the bins.

"Ina Dudley?" she whispered.

The woman spun around, and Kerise raised her hands.

"Who are you?"

"I'm from Asteria. I came to talk to you about a letter you sent in."

The woman glanced back at the house. "That was years ago," she hissed. "Before I was married. Please leave."

"I need to speak to you about Selene Richards."

Ina stepped backwards and pulled the front door closed, throwing both of them into darkness.

"Come," she whispered, and Kerise followed her around the side of the house.

Ina stopped where a small extension joined the main house, and crushed herself into the corner. She crouched, lifted a flower pot, and pulled out a packet of cigarettes. She slipped a lighter from the packet and lit one, the momentary flare of the flame illuminating her taut face. The glow of the cigarette bobbed up and down as she spoke.

"I was married shortly after sending the letter, so I never even saw if it was published. Or if Asteria replied. I think Selene's been sending out messages, randomly, hoping someone will pick them up. Like radio broadcasts. I suspect there are other women who could hear them too."

"What did she say?"

"It's patchy. Disjointed words and images. Like interference. She sent names, but they meant nothing to me. Lots of words I didn't even recognise. I kept a diary of them. I thought they might be important one day."

"When was the last one?"

The cigarette's glow blazed as Ina inhaled. "They became far less frequent over the years, and weaker. I haven't heard from her in about eighteen months."

"Do you think she's still alive?"

There was a moment of silence. "Yes I do. But I don't know for how much longer."

"Did you send any messages back?"

"At first, but I don't know if she got them. If she did, she never showed any sign of having done so.

She might be up there thinking no one's listening to her at all."

"Up there?"

"In The Eye."

"She's definitely there?"

"Yes. She sent me a vision of the staircase, and the stone lions perched at the top of it."

"Can I have your diary?"

"Yes, of course. But it's hidden in the house. I'll meet you tomorrow, when my husband's at work. I'll meet you on The Hope. Do you know the Dandelion Tap on Navel Street?"

"The little tea shop, yes, I know it."

"I'll meet you there at eleven."

Kerise ordered another tea and glanced up at the clock behind the counter. Numbers one to eleven were represented by cups and saucers, and the twelve was a slice of cake topped with cream and a strawberry. The hour hand was a teaspoon, the minute hand a cake fork. Kerise winced.

She folded her soft pink paper napkin as many times as she could, making the square of it smaller and thicker. She tried to fold it an eighth time, but the paper refused. She knew it was impossible, but she kept trying, just in case she found a way to beat the odds. After all, beating the odds was what she did. The woman with more lives than a cat.

She couldn't count the number of times she'd dodged a bullet, or had a knife at her throat. She should be long dead. But it never slowed her down, it simply spurred her on with more proof that she was invincible.

Her tea came, and she idly stirred it. Ina was almost an hour late, and if Kerise kept handing over drinks credits, they would start to get suspicious.

She sat and watched women come and go, women banned from working, barred from having any purpose in life until the day of their marriage. Kerise was lucky to have found her own purpose.

She pushed back her chair and walked out, leaving her tea untouched.

Kerise hovered outside the tea shop, considering whether to go to Ina's house. Deciding against it, she turned towards Eye Street and The Paper Duchess.

42

"There was nothing wrong with her," Jonas York told the group of men. "It was all in her head. It was the medicine that killed her, the very thing she thought would make her better. But it was poison."

One man lifted his arm and shooed him away.

"Look," another said, "I'm sorry you lost your wife, but we're just trying to have a quiet lunch before the afternoon shift. Go tell your sad story to someone else."

"But we need to be doing something about this. Please." Jonas reached out and touched the first man's arm.

He pulled away and jumped to his feet, his chair clattering to the floor. "Just back off!" He pushed Jonas, and laughed as Jonas stumbled into the table behind him.

Reva swept over, and talked the man back into his seat with gentle coos and apologies. She gathered Jonas up, and led him back to the bar. She poured him another drink. On the house.

"No one's listening to me," Jonas said. "They don't care."

"They didn't know Fay, this isn't their story. You can't interrupt people's meals and expect them to join your cause."

"But this is everyone's cause. That man's selling poison to the population of Falside. How many people might have died already?"

Reva nodded. "I know. But we need to go about this another way. Cora confirmed that she found hemlock in the bottle, and that Fay's death matched hemlock poisoning. She's a respected herbologist on The Floor, people will listen to her. She's spreading the word among her customers—"

"But they already get their medicines from her, they're not the ones buying from the apothecary."

"I know, but her customers are women, and if you want to spread information, it's the female grapevine that moves it fastest. Women will tell their friends, who will tell their friends. They'll tell their husbands, and those that listen will go to work and tell their workmates. This will spread, Jonas, but harassing people isn't the way to do things."

"So we just sit back and wait for more people to die? More families to be torn apart?"

Reva placed her hand over Jonas'. "Justice will be done."

"I just..." Jonas shook his head. "I can't just sit back and do nothing. Maybe the grapevine will do its thing, but I can't rely on it."

He finished his drink in a couple of gulps and skulked out of The Burnt Scroll. Stumbling down the road, he slipped into the next public house. He ordered a drink for more courage, and started moving from table to table.

"You have to listen to me, more people are going to die."

"Just leave us alone."

"You're drunk. Or crazy. Get out of here."

"It could be your wife next," Jonas called out to the whole room. "Or your parents, or your children. By doing nothing, you're as guilty as the apothecary."

Jonas felt two strong hands clasp around his arms. He was lifted off his feet and carried outside, where he was unceremoniously dumped onto the ground.

"Don't you come back," the landlord said. He spat a globule of spittle onto Jonas' leg. "Bloody drunkard."

He received the same reception everywhere. Indifference from the patrons, and expulsion from the owners.

Until he found himself stood outside the apothecary. He stared up at it, swaying from side to side, blinking to focus his vision.

"He's selling poison," he told the people passing by. Barely anyone even glanced at him. "He's poisoning people. With hemlock."

He stumbled, reaching out, and bracing himself against a man's shoulder. The man took hold of him, and gently eased him to the ground.

"You should go home. Sleep it off," he said.

Jonas shook his head madly. "I have to warn people."

"Warn people of what?"

Jonas gestured at the apothecary shop. "He's selling poison."

"It's medicine. Sure it tastes awful, but it's medicine."

Jonas shook his head again, the world wheeling around him. "There's hemlock in it. It's poisonous. Kills people within hours." He touched his chest. "They can't breathe. They die. They just die."

"Let's get you home," the man said, helping Jonas to his feet.

"Why won't anyone listen?"

"Sober up, come back tomorrow. I'm sure you'll be seeing things more clearly then."

"Why won't they listen?"

"You're drunk, people will think you're just rambling. Come back sober. You'll see things for what they really are."

Jonas waggled his finger at the man. "You're right. People will believe me when I'm sober. You're right."

"Do you know your way home?"

Jonas nodded. "I just follow my broken heart."

43

Harris watched the man stumble away down the street. He probably should have seen him home, but he had more important things on his mind than the ravings of a drunk.

He climbed the steps to the apothecary and pushed the door open.

Lou looked up from his newspaper.

"My God, what happened to you?" Harris asked.

"Your bloody daughter," Lou said. "It's not good for business, me looking like this."

"Maeve did that to you? A small, slight seventeen year old girl?"

"She'll be punished when it all stops hurting."

Harris crossed to the counter. "Leave her alone, Lou. She stood up to you for once, and it's no more than you deserve. It's no more than you've ever deserved. You've hit women around your entire life, it's about time one of them fought back."

"You think you're so righteous."

Harris drew himself up straight. "Where's my daughter, Lou?"

"God only knows. We keep out of each other's way these days."

"Good. Keep it that way." Harris tapped the desk, turned, and walked through the door to the hall. The kitchen was empty, so he trundled upstairs and gently tapped on Maeve's door.

"Go away," came her voice from inside.

"It's Father Harris." He cleared his throat. "It's your dad."

Harris listened as something big and heavy was pulled away from the door. The handle turned, and Maeve's face appeared.

"What do you want?"

"You're barricading yourself in?"

"Do I have a choice?" She smiled slightly. "Did you see Uncle Lou?"

Harris nodded.

"Are you angry?"

Harris reached out and ruffled Maeve's hair. "I'm proud of you, sweetheart." The unfamiliar word sounded awkward in his mouth, but she smiled back at him, and opened the door further.

Harris pushed past the bed and into the room. He looked at the door. "Do you want me to put a bolt on this for you?"

"Would you?"

"Sure." He sat on the edge of the bed. "I know I've totally screwed things up right now, but I want to be someone you can come to, even grow to trust and rely on. I'm ready to do this."

"I'm almost eighteen."

"And you've proven yourself to be very capable. Wow, you must've really laid into your uncle." He laughed. "He'll think twice before laying a hand on you again."

"It won't last long. The bruises will fade, and he'll be back to his old self."

Harris looked at his hands in his lap. He clenched and flexed them. "I thought I'd found a way to get you out of the city, but it was too dangerous. I want to make things better for you, Maeve, I really do. You shouldn't have to be barricading yourself into your bedroom. I'm going to find somewhere for you to go."

"Do you really mean that? Or are you just going to abandon me again?"

"I really mean it. I've got a lot to set right, and I'm starting with you." He stood up. "Let me buy you lunch. When was the last time you had a proper meal?"

Maeve hesitated.

"Come on. One meal."

She nodded and followed him out of the room. They trailed down the stairs and into the shop.

"I am taking my daughter out to lunch," Harris announced.

Lou watched them leave, his face set in a scowl.

"He hates to see anything good happening for me," Maeve whispered as they descended the steps to the street.

"Is that what I am? Something good?"

"You better be. You saw what I did to Uncle Lou."

They laughed.

As they wandered down The Wall, Harris began to relax. Maeve seemed content to be with him; something he couldn't have imagined after their first meeting.

They reached the steps up to The Hope, and Maeve slowed, veering towards them. Harris caught her hand.

"I found a nice café further along The Wall I thought we'd go to."

Maeve frowned. "The slums? You're not taking me up to The Hope?"

Harris shifted his weight. "No."

"Our first time out together, and you're taking me to a slum café?"

Harris looked up the street, and chewed on his lip. He looked back at Maeve.

"Look, I'm a monk, and there are certain expectations. A big one of them being celibacy. I can't really parade you around up there announcing that you're my daughter. I was already a novice when you were born. You understand, right?"

Maeve backed away. "Sure I understand. You're ashamed of me. You're ashamed of your illegitimate slum-girl of a daughter." Maeve raised her voice and people began to stare. "Down here I can be your daughter, but up there?" She gestured at the steps. "Up there I'm just a sordid little secret. Yes, I understand perfectly well."

She turned, and marched away.

For a moment, Harris considered going after her, but there was really only one way he was going to fix this. Hitching up his habit, Harris set off up the steps, fully aware of the eyes on him.

44

Tale stared harder at the screen in front of her. Denver had been whistling his way around his mountainous landscape of books for almost forty minutes, and it was driving her nuts. She didn't even know what he did in there all day. He seemed to just shift books around; from one pile to another, then back again. He claimed to have a system, but no one else could see it.

Besides, it wasn't as if he ever had customers. Maybe once a week someone would wander in, often by accident, usually buying a book out of sheer embarrassment. It was a horrible feeling to be the only customer in any shop. That feeling of enormous duty.

The shop was just a front, a façade. It was a convenient mask for what really went on at The Paper Duchess. After all, who would want to come poking around in the back rooms if they first had to navigate the narrow gulleys and ravines of the book shop. It was a daunting enough task for Tale, and one that Kerise chose to avoid altogether.

Tale shook her head and attempted to bring the words in front of her back into focus. She'd had a letter from yet another conspiracy theorist, but the

Asteria was committed to giving everyone's ideas a fair shot, however crazy.

She'd lost count of the number of letters that claimed the reason so few girls were being born was because of aliens. That was a pretty common theory. Then there was poisonous air, poisonous food, poisonous water. One person had even claimed that, because life for women was so restrictive and depressing, they had found a way to will themselves to only have boys, who were destined for a far better existence. Actually, Tale liked to think that one was true; women retaliating against their oppression in the only way they knew how.

Tale winced as the whistling grew louder. She hadn't had nearly enough coffee yet to cope with Denver's infuriatingly constant good moods.

"Post," he chirruped as he entered the room. He dumped a few letters and a slim parcel onto Tale's desk. "What you working on?"

"Exactly," Tale replied.

"Huh?"

She turned her chair around to face him. "Exactly, Denver, I'm working, and your incessant whistling and pottering about isn't helping."

Denver didn't seem to get the hint as he grabbed a chair and settled himself down.

"What's this one?" he asked.

Tale sighed. "Another theory, although this one's a little better thought through than the others. Rather than just ignoring it because it doesn't fit their idea, they've actually addressed the question of why the girl boy birth ratio is perfectly normal in the slums, but totally out of balance in the rest of Falside."

"How's that?"

"What's one of the major things that slums don't have that we do?"

Denver shrugged.

"A shared water supply," Tale said. "In the slums they largely use rainwater, or some people filter river water. But up here, one water supply controlled by the administration. So if they found a way, chemically, to restrict the production of sperm carrying the X chromosome, and administered it through our drinking water, the slums would be unaffected."

"Do you think they have the knowledge and the technology to create something like that?"

"Who knows? I've never heard of anything like that, but no one knows what goes on up in The Eye. They could be doing all sorts."

"But this? It's a bit science fiction, isn't it?"

"Once upon a time the car was science fiction, or the computer. Remember, as a population, we've regressed. We've abandoned technology and chosen to move backwards."

"Because the administration spied on us twenty four seven."

"Exactly." Tale leaned back in her chair. "Maybe that was their plan all along. We've forgotten just how far, technologically, humans had come, and how fast we were developing. I mean, look at this." She pulled back her wrist to reveal her

ID stamp, embedded deep into her skin. "A century ago, this was science fiction. We've forgotten just how much humans are capable of."

Denver frowned, processing his thoughts. "Still, it could just be another crazy theory."

"Absolutely."

"Besides, why would any leadership want to vigorously control the weaker half of the population?"

Tale grinned and stood up. She patted Denver on the shoulder as she made her way to the kettle for a caffeine refill.

"My poor dumb boy, because women aren't the weaker sex. We create life, and that makes us both all-powerful, and completely terrifying. We can do something men couldn't even physically survive. If you control women, you control the birth rate. And if you control that, you control the whole population."

Tale waited for the kettle to boil, drumming her fingers against the worktop.

"And you find my whistling annoying," Denver said.

"This is caffeine-induced, yours is just your annoying personality." Tale grinned over her shoulder at him, but she was only half joking.

"Let's see what other crazy batshit came in the post today then." Denver grabbed the pile of post and looked through it, shuffling the envelopes like a deck of cards. Discarding the letters back to the desk, he turned the parcel over in his hands.

Tale watched him with increasing infuriation. Thankfully the kettle clicked, and her mug was filled with a drug-induced cheery mood. Well, as cheery as her mood ever got.

She turned back to Denver who appeared to be sniffing the package. She strode over, and snatched it from his hands.

"God only knows where that's been. Go and wash your damn face. Besides, this is my post."

"It feels like a book," Denver said, as if that gave him some kind of ownership over it.

"Oh, that's why you've got all excited and sweaty." She dropped it onto the desk. "Maybe I'll open it later." She enjoyed watching him, quite literally, squirm in his seat. She sipped at her coffee, blowing the steam from the top of it.

"Does it really pain you that much?" she asked.

"It's a book, a book. How can it not pain you?"

Tale grinned and put down her mug. She picked up the packet and turned it over. There was nothing written on the back, and only Asteria written on the front. It had been hurriedly written; the word fading into no more than a squiggle. She shook it.

"It's a book," Denver cried.

"Alright, alright." Tale slipped her thumb under the flap and pulled the glue apart. She slid it out into her hand. It was a hard-back notebook, dark blue. She looked into the envelope and pulled out a note. "You have what you wanted. Never come to my house again," she read.

"Is it that woman's diary?" Denver asked. "The one that was meant to meet Kerise."

Tale flipped the book open and scanned a few pages. "Looks like it."

"What does it say?" Denver rose from his chair, trying to peer at it.

Tale twisted away from him and flipped further through. "This is going to take a while to decipher. The woman wasn't kidding, it really is just snippets and random thoughts. Oh, here's Maeve's name. And her uncle. Yeah, this is going to be a long job."

"Do you need some help?"

The last thing Tale wanted was to spend the rest of the day with Denver sat next to her. He oozed happiness, it radiated from him like heat waves. But she was behind schedule with the current issue, and this diary was a distraction she didn't need.

"Alright," she conceded. "But you should find Kerise, she's going to want to see this."

45

Lino Calderon had buried his wife less than a year ago. She died of tuberculosis, leaving him to raise their four year old daughter alone.

His daughter was the absolute image of his late wife, and she grew more like her every day. Lino worshipped her, keeping his wife's memory alive in her innocent and curious eyes.

Still grieving his loss, Lino was an over-protective and cautious parent, forever telling his daughter what she couldn't do, couldn't touch, couldn't put in her mouth. He was a regular at the doctor's surgery, always worried about something with his daughter. A rash, tiredness, tantrums, grazed knees. But the doctor was sympathetic, and always took the time to reassure him, rather than simply sending him away.

That morning, Lino's daughter woke with a cough. Terrified that it was tuberculosis, Lino hurried her to the doctor.

It so happened that the doctor's eldest daughter was getting married. It was something they never imagined would happen. She was a plain girl, with little personality and no hobbies or interests, and all of her younger sisters had been married several years already.

He had taken a rare day off work for the joyous family occasion.

Lino was offered a different doctor. This doctor was far younger, and an argument with his wife this morning had left him feeling on edge, and impatient. He swiftly sent Lino away with a severe reprimand for having wasted his time.

Desperate with worry, Lino had stopped by the apothecary shop and purchased a particularly expensive bottle of medicine. The apothecary had assured him that he would get no better cure for tuberculosis.

When Lino arrived home with his daughter, he put her straight to bed, and gave her a generous dose of medicine. He then cleaned and tidied the kitchen; a habit that always calmed his nerves, as it had his mother before him.

Over the clattering of pots and pans, and the chinking of crockery, he didn't hear his daughter suffocating.

When he checked on her an hour later, she was as cold and dead as winter.

April Terrell hadn't meant to get pregnant. She hadn't even meant to fall in love, particularly with her married boss. But he was older, sophisticated, and knew all the right things to say. In fact, he had said all the right things to his previous six secretaries.

April had spent her youth with her nose in books. Her mother had always told her that no good would ever come of all that reading, but she devoured stories like they were the only things keeping her alive. She loved the way everyone lived happily ever after, and came to believe that she would live happily ever after herself. How could she not? Everyone did.

Sadly, her mother had been right. April had grown into a naïve woman who was too quick to trust. She wore her heart on her sleeve, and she fell in love hard and fast. Despite many heartbreaks over the years, she had failed to develop any sense of cynicism or cautiousness.

That, in itself, should be a beautiful thing and, in a perfect world, we should all live like that. But this was not a perfect world, and there were always people willing to take advantage of people like April.

When April had informed her boss of her situation, he had gone through a series of emotions. At first he denied it, accusing her of cheating, of sleeping around. Then he grew fearful, followed by anger, but when the bruise he left on her cheekbone began to darken, he moved into guilt and regret.

Fearful that his wife would find out about yet another misdemeanour, he explained that he would have to ask April to quit. He promised her a sizeable severance packet, and hush money, on the understanding that she sign a non-disclosure agreement absolving him of any parental duty.

Certain that this was brought on by fear, April signed it, and took the money, convinced that they would tear it up when he finally got over the shock, saw sense, and left his wife for her.

Seven months on, she still hadn't heard from him, and she was beginning to think he might not see sense after all.

She was already an attentive and loving mother, following strict health, exercise, and dietary regimes to assure the very best start for her unborn child. She talked to it, sang to it, and that baby was her entire world. She couldn't wait to meet it.

Throughout the pregnancy, April had suffered from worsening heartburn, and had added so many extra pillows to her bed that she was almost sleeping upright. The only thing to soothe it was milk, but this wasn't cheap in the slums. Falside's rocky terrain made it difficult to graze cows, and most of the city's milk supply was imported.

April's severance pay was beginning to run out, and she could no longer afford to buy the generous milk supply she needed. After four days of sleepless nights, she sought the help of an apothecary, who sold her medicine to relieve her heartburn.

Sleep deprived and exhausted, April fell into a deep sleep with her stomach full of medicine. She never woke up.

She was found two days later by her neighbour who popped in now and again to check on her. The neighbour didn't know her well enough to say for sure if she had any family that needed to be informed. She put a notice in the local paper, but it went unanswered.

46

Harris had been stood outside the abbot's door for almost half an hour trying to pluck up the courage to knock on it.

He had run the conversation through his head a hundred times, all with different outcomes, ranging from joyous hugs and congratulations, to either himself or the abbot ending up dead.

Harris raised his hand again, and drew Maeve's face into his mind. This time, his hand made contact with the wood, albeit lightly. He waited, hoping the abbot hadn't heard him knock.

"Come," bellowed a voice from within.

The abbot was one of the oldest men Harris had ever seen. His face was like a used, dried teabag, topped with just a dusting of hair, but finished off with a long and wiry beard. The beard almost entirely obscured the man's mouth, and curled up around his nose as if it hoped to, one day, join with his impressive eyebrows.

"Father Harris," the abbot said, not rising from his seat.

Harris wondered how many years he'd been

stuck in that chair.

"Abbot." Harris bowed his head. "I come to you with a distressing confession that I can no longer keep to myself."

The abbot gestured to the chair, and Harris sat.

"I need to confess to you of a sin I committed seventeen years ago, when I was just a novice here."

The abbot leaned forward. Something creaked, but Harris wasn't sure if it was the chair, or the old man's spine.

"Abbot, I have a daughter."

The abbot coughed. The cough got worse, until the old man was convulsing with it. Harris picked up a glass of water from the desk, but the abbot shooed it away.

When he stopped coughing, Harris caught sight of his teeth amongst the overgrown beard, and wondered if the man had, in fact, been laughing.

"Congratulations," he said. "At least you managed to produce a girl."

"I'm not in trouble?" Harris asked.

The abbot shook his head. "Most of the monks have a child running around somewhere, more than one in most cases. I myself am the father of an impressive horde of bastards. But—" The abbot pushed his forefinger against the top of the desk. "—I must be seen to do something. Keep up appearances."

"I understand."

"I think some time of silent prayer and reflection will be suitable. And some charitable work, perhaps a children's charity. Be seen. Be remorseful. Let people know that you are keen to repay your debt."

"Can I bring my daughter to The Hope?"

The abbot nodded slowly. "Be discreet. I don't require you to lie about her paternity, but don't shout about it. Keep her out of church business, and offer her no perks. That should do fine."

"Thank you, Abbot." Harris bowed his head.

"Is that all?"

"Yes."

The abbot gestured towards the door.

Harris stood and smoothed down his habit. He bowed again and crossed to the door. As he pulled it open, the abbot spoke again.

"Perhaps one day you'll confess to me about the dead hooker you buried in the garden. Or why you dug her back up again."

Harris walked into the apothecary, headed for the hall without even glancing at Lou.

"Back again?" Lou said. "And not even a hello this time?"

Harris stopped, and turned to him. "I am trying to build a relationship with my daughter."

"So, is this going to be a weekly thing now? Just so that I know. I could roll out the red carpet next time."

"Shut up, Louis." Harris moved for the door, but stopped when Lou spoke again.

"I don't think she'll want to see you."

Harris turned back to him, and folded his arms across his chest. "And what do you know about what she wants?"

"Because I had to listen to her bloody crying all night after the last time you were here. It was a very short lunch, Harris."

"Watch out, you almost sound like you care."

Lou grinned. "What's all this self-righteousness? Turned over a new leaf, have we? Rediscovered God?"

"I'm trying to put things right with my daughter."

"You mean the daughter you dumped with me seventeen years ago and didn't bother about until the other week? That daughter? Selene's blood is on your hands too, don't you forget that."

Harris lowered his arms, slipping his hands behind his back. "I've not forgotten."

Lou huffed. "Is that man still outside?"

"What man?"

"Shouting nonsense about me being a murderer or something. Just some crazy arse. Bad for business though."

Harris smiled. "He's there. And he's picked up a few new disciples too."

As Lou rushed to the window, Harris continued through to the hall and up the stairs.

He tapped on Maeve's door. "I have a big apology to make, don't I?"

There was movement inside the room, the creak of the bed. "I wouldn't bother," came Maeve's voice from the other side of the door.

"I thought we could go and buy a bolt for your door. There's a nice little hardware shop up on The Hope."

"Did you honestly think it would be that easy?"

"I told the abbot about you."

"Excuse me if I don't applaud."

"I want to take you to the monastery and introduce you to everyone. I want to show off my beautiful daughter."

The door opened a crack. "It's my forgiveness you're meant to be seeking, not the abbot's."

"That's what I'm trying to do."

"Too late."

"Then tell me what I need to do."

"I shouldn't have to."

Harris rolled his eyes. "We'll do whatever you want on The Hope. Get coffee, eat chocolate, have a meal. I'll show you the monastery gardens. Most people don't get to see them."

The door opened a little further. "You're bribing me with sweets? I'm not six anymore."

Harris placed his hand on the door and gently pushed it open further. "I know you're not. But I owe you a whole lifetime's worth."

Harris poked his head into the room. Maeve had moved to the far wall.

"I screwed up. Big time. Again. I'm a crap father, and I always have been. But if you'll let me try to make it up to you, I'd like the chance to do that."

Maeve turned away, and looked out of the window.

"What else would you be doing today?"

Maeve shrugged, and turned back to him. "You're on probation."

"Of course, of course." He held his hand out to her. After a moment, she crossed the room, and let him help her over the bed. As she climbed back down, he caught sight of dark bruises up her legs. She saw him looking.

"Courtesy of my uncle."

"Let's get you out of here."

47

Maeve felt a lot safer now that she had a bolt on her door. Uncle Lou had stopped opening the shop. There hadn't been any custom for several days, and the horde of angry people outside was growing steadily. They shouted and screamed all day, accusing Lou of being a murderer, using hemlock to poison innocent people. She could hear Lou pacing around the house, she could feel his frustration growing. He couldn't risk facing the mob outside.

Maeve crossed to the window and looked down. There were even more of them today, and some of them had brought improvised weapons; wooden batons, chair legs, bricks. One of them threw something at the door, the thud shaking up through the building. Maeve looked down and saw red paint splattered everywhere.

She spun around as someone knocked on her bedroom door.

"Maeve! Maeve!" It was Uncle Lou.

"What?" she shouted back.

"They're trying to get in. What do we do?"

"They threw something at the door, they're not trying to get in." She glanced back out of the window. The crowd was growing. People liked to be part of something, to belong to a group, even if they didn't fully understand, or care, what that group was about.

She crossed the room, slid back the bolt, and opened her door.

Uncle Lou was a shadow. Even thinner than he was before, and his face still displayed the final yellows of the bruises. His eyes were sunken, his stature hunched. Maeve almost felt sorry for the man. Almost.

"We need to leave," she said. "We need to get to the monastery. Harris will protect us."

Lou marched into the room. "If I go out there, they'll tear me limb from limb."

"We need to go now before it gets to that."

"I'm not leaving."

"Then we're just sitting ducks, waiting for them to come in and get us. So, you stay here if you want, I'm leaving."

She moved towards the door, but Lou grabbed her wrist and tugged her back. She stumbled, and fell backwards. Lou kept hold of her wrist, and her head snapped back, and slammed into the floor. Her vision flashed.

She heard Lou shifting around, she heard him leave the room, climb the stairs, pull his bed in front of the door. And then her attention shifted to the people outside.

She could almost feel the emotions of each of

them, her mind reaching out like fingers. They were angry, scared, grief-stricken, excited. She could feel their intentions.

Maeve lay flat on her back on the hard floor. Maeve's eyes were closed. Maeve's mouth was smiling.

48

Tale leaned against the worktop and sipped her fresh coffee. Denver and Kerise were still studying the diary. They had written several sheets of notes, interpretations, trying to patch snippets together to build a picture.

"Look at this," said Kerise, passing the diary to Denver. She pointed to the page. "Is that what I think it is?"

Denver frowned as he read it. He nodded.

"Now can we get her out of there?" Kerise asked.

Tale stepped forward. "What is it?"

"It's a prophecy," Kerise said, "of Maeve's death."

49

Maeve felt the horde decide. She felt them start to move. Before they began smashing at the front door, she knew they were coming.

She heard the door splinter, she heard it surrender, and the feet and the hands clawed the wooden shards out of their way. She heard the bottles breaking in the shop, the counter being overturned.

They moved into the kitchen, pulling everything apart, and smashing furniture to arm themselves. They found knives, and skewers. And then, curled into a bucket, they found the murder weapon. They overturned the barrel in the storage room and smashed the empty bottles. They found the hemlock.

"Here it is!" they yelled triumphantly, as if they had still wanted proof before carrying out what they had in mind. They threw it to the floor and ground it beneath their boots.

Then they started up the stairs.

They tore the bathroom apart, smashed the porcelain, and sent jets of water into the air. They peered into Maeve's bedroom, but didn't spot the skinny, bruised legs sticking out from behind the bed.

They continued upstairs.

They pushed against Lou's bedroom door, they hammered, they yelled.

"We'll get you, you murderous bastard!"

"You won't get the chance to kill any more innocent people!"

"You'll get just what you deserve!"

Maeve heard the bedroom door splinter, and she heard furniture being pushed out of the way.

"String him up! String the bastard up!"

"The hangman's jig!"

"Please, please, I didn't do anything. It's just dirty water. I'm a fraud, but I'm not a murderer. I don't know anything about the hemlock, I don't even know what it looks like. Please."

Maeve reached out with her mind. She could feel the rope, wound around into a noose, taut, expectant. She felt it around Lou's neck, heavy and rough. It chafed his skin as the horde pulled him this way and that. Cats playing with their prey.

"Please. It wasn't me. It was the girl. She bottled the medicine. She gathered the plants. It was the girl! The girl!"

The bed squealed across the floor as Uncle Lou was tossed from the window. When the bed frame hit the wall, the rope pulled taut. His body slammed into the front of the building, his leg banging against Maeve's window frame. She squealed.

And then the horde had a new intention.

"Where's the girl?"

Maeve struggled to her feet, her head spinning. She staggered to the door, but they were already down the stairs. She slammed it shut, her fingers fumbling over the bolt. She slipped, tried again, and finally slid it closed. She stumbled backwards as hands slammed into the wood, feet, shoulders, improvised clubs and battering rams.

The wood began to splinter, like a mouth grinning across the door. The mouth widened, bearing its wooden teeth.

Maeve looked around the bare room desperately. Her face ran with sweat, her hands slipped from everything she touched.

A cool breeze hit her, chilling her damp skin. She spun around. A hand reached out to her, and she instinctively took it. She was whisked out of the window and onto the roof.

"They were going to kill me too," she whispered as she was carried over the rooftops.

50

When Maeve woke, she was dry and warm. Her head ached, but at least she could see straight. She was lying on a mat, covered with a blanket. She looked up at the vaulted ceiling above her.

She could hear people moving around, talking in hushed voices.

Maeve pushed herself upright, her head protesting. Her mouth was dry, her muscles were tired. She smiled. The pain meant that she was alive.

She tested her legs, and they seemed willing to support her. She wandered out of the room and into a corridor. Following the sound of the voices, and the smell of coffee, she shuffled along, running one hand along the wall.

She stopped at an open doorway and looked in. One woman sat at a computer, another was lounging in a chair next to her. Another was sat cross-legged on the worktop.

"You're up." The woman climbed down from the worktop in a smooth motion. Cat-like. "How are you feeling?"

"Aching. And a little confused," Maeve said. She cleared her throat.

"Then have some coffee, because we have a lot of explaining to do."

"Where am I?"

"You're safe. You're in The Paper Duchess."

The woman pulled out a chair, and urged Maeve to sit.

She gestured to herself. "I'm Kerise." To the woman at the computer. "That's Tale." And to the third woman. "And Freda. You'll meet Denver later."

Kerise handed Maeve a mug, and Maeve wrapped her hands around it; the warm drink an instant comfort.

"You saved me?" Maeve asked.

Kerise nodded. "I did."

"How did you know?"

Kerise smiled. "Your mother told us."

EPILOGUE

Harris stepped back and shielded his eyes against the sun. He watched the man unhook the apothecary sign, and pass it down to his colleague. His colleague passed him the new sign and he latched it onto the bracket. He turned to Harris, who nodded his approval. The man descended the ladder.

"That's us done," he said. "You're all ready to open up shop."

"Thank you," Harris said. He counted out the agreed credits and handed them over.

Harris stepped towards the new front door, painted a sunny yellow, and stepped inside. The apothecary shop, once lined with shelves and bottles of stinking water, was now a bright café. Tables were dotted around, each boasting three chairs and a yellow table cloth. Flowers adorned the window ledges and the counter.

On the wall behind the counter, sweeping black letters spelled out a re-purposed motto. It read; 'Our duty is friendship. Our role is love. This is your freedom.'

Harris wandered back to the kitchen. He looked into the storeroom, now decked with shelves and filled with food, blankets, clothing. The kitchen was clean and airy, filled with the scent of lemons.

Upstairs, Maeve's bedroom had a line of beds, each one neatly made, awaiting guests. The bathroom was crisp and white. Lou's bedroom also boasted several beds. Each one had a small cot beside it. The walls were painted white, and the room was filled with sunshine.

Harris smiled, and fought back the tears. It was exactly what she would have wanted, and the perfect memorial.

Harris walked back downstairs. The women had arrived, and the kitchen was filled with chatter, laughter, and the happy clanging of pots and pans.

He walked back through the café and out into the warm air. He looked up at the sign as it swung gently back and forth.

Lacey's House.
A sanctuary for the women of Falside.

ABOUT ANGELINE TREVENA

Angeline Trevena was born and bred in a rural corner of Devon, but now lives among the breweries and canals of central England with her husband, son, and a rather neurotic cat. She is a horror and fantasy writer, poet, and journalist.

In 2003 she graduated from Edge Hill University, Lancashire, with a BA Hons Degree in Drama and Writing. During this time she decided that her future lay in writing words rather than performing them.

Some years ago she worked at an antique auction house and religiously checked every wardrobe that came in to see if Narnia was in the back of it. She's still not given up looking for it.

Find out more at www.angelinetrevena.co.uk

ACKNOWLEDGEMENTS

I want to thank my family for their unconditional support and endless patience. My husband who seems to believe in me more than I do, our son whose long afternoon naps have granted me the time to write. My very talented brother, Ben, who knows me well enough to smash the design brief first time to produce a cover I am immeasurably proud of. My sister, Heidi, for her critical eye, even when it faltered in the face of a gripping story. My wonderful and invaluable beta readers; Anthony Redden, Tony Benson, and Pixie Peigh; for their time, their kind words, and their honest ones too. Louise Yoxall who allowed me to borrow her likeness and character traits for Topley. My fellow writers who have supported and championed me, and given me endless amounts of their time and knowledge. Everyone who has believed in me, and supported me on this journey, even in ways they don't realise. This wouldn't have been possible without them.